Rose C. Falls

Cheniere Caminada

The wind of death - The story of the storm in Louisiana

Rose C. Falls

Cheniere Caminada
The wind of death - The story of the storm in Louisiana

ISBN/EAN: 9783337403676

Printed in Europe, USA, Canada, Australia, Japan

Cover: Foto ©Andreas Hilbeck / pixelio.de

More available books at **www.hansebooks.com**

CHENIERE ❊ CAMINADA

— OR —

THE WIND OF DEATH.

THE STORY OF THE STORM IN LOUISIANA.

By ROSE C. FALLS.

NEW ORLEANS:

HOPKINS' PRINTING OFFICE, 20 & 22 COMMERCIAL PLACE.

1893.

TO

ROBERT BLEAKLEY,

CHAIRMAN OF THE CITIZENS' RELIEF

COMMITTEE,

and his colleagues, members of that Committee,

whose prompt action, untiring energy

and generous humanity will ever

be blessed by the helpless and

homeless,

This Work is Respectfully Dedicated

— BY —

THE AUTHOR.

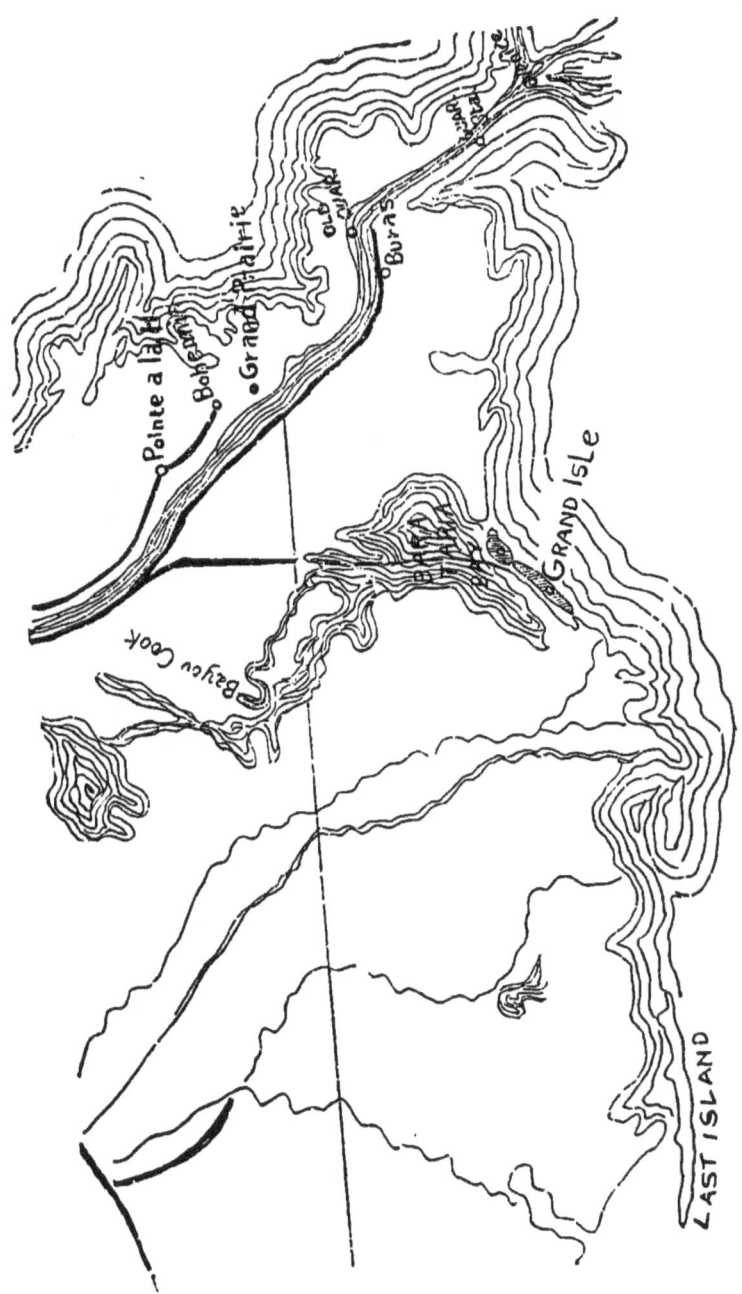

CHAPTER I.

The gulf coast of Louisiana, that stretch of level sea marsh and sluggish bayou, is rich in song and story. It lives in the pages of both romance and history, and fact and fancy are so interwoven there that they cannot be separated. The pitiful story of Evangeline reads like fact, while the true tale of the whispering sands of Pascagoula sounds like the wildest flight of fancy. It was on this coast that was made one of the only two landings on our shores of a foreign foe; and from its low-lying islands came the pirate Lafitte to offer his services, in her hour of peril, to his country, which had proscribed him for his crimes in the time of peace. But these islands of the coast have changed since the days of Lafitte. The "long, low, rakish schooner," has been replaced by the lugger of the oysterman, and the inhabitants are hardy fisherman, "toilers of the sea," instead of black bearded free-booters of the deep. Those who peopled these islands and the adjacent coasts were of almost every race and nation of the earth. The Anglo-Saxon, the Malay, the Creole, the Negro, the Austrian, the Italian, the Chinaman, the Spaniard, the German, were all to be found there.

There they reared their "camps," or fishing huts, on piles to have them beyond the reach of the high spring tides; there they brought their wives and reared their children and made that "home," which every man, no matter what his race, must have. The blue waters of the gulf was the field of their labor, and the city of New Orleans, a half a hundred miles away, and reached by way of the tortuous bayous, was the market for their finny spoil.

A sturdy, happy people they were, strong in their affections, proud in their self-reliance, open-hearted in their hospitality, ready to share, with the needy, their substance, and asking naught save a just return for their hard and often dangerous labor.

As the population increased it naturally grouped itself into communities, and Grand Isle, Cheniere Caminada, Grand Terre, and the many other fishing settlements in what was collectively known as "the Barataria Country," were the result.

Sunday, October 1st, 1893, dawned upon this section of Louisiana, and the sun rose,

"Not, as in northern climes. obscurely bright,
But one unclouded blaze of living light,"

and it ne'er shown on people happier or more peaceful. Fishing tackle and all the implements of week day toil were put aside, and the bronzed fishermen enjoyed the sweet association of their wives and little ones.

The Gulf was uncommonly smooth—no breath raised a ripple on its surface, but there was a ceaseless, gentle swell, as if, amid the coral beds beneath, some lonely water spirit slumbered, while the waters above rose and fell with its steady breathing. From the swamps about the morning songs of myriads of birds ascended, as they flitted to and fro among the moss draped trees, and when the Sun rose higher in the Heavens the waters of the currentless bayous were parted by the heads of lazy alligators, that came to the surface to wink and blink at the sunshine.

There was enrapturing consonance of sound and sight, of woodland song and sea shore scenery. It was a morning to kindle a poet's fancy—calm and unruffled as a martyr's mind, and bright as the hope that animates his bosom. But as the day waned, the scene was changed. Clouds chased each other across the blue of the Heavens and grew darker and more angry looking as the evening approached. The shadows in the swamps grew black and the murmuring of the moss draped limbs of the trees grew louder and louder. Sea birds skimmed across the water and sent forth frightened cries. The alligators sank to the bottom of the bayous, and the birds sought their nests with plaintive trills. The fishermen gathered their loved ones into the shelter of their homes and said: "a storm is brewing."

But little they knew the devastation that would be the result of that storm to which they so carelessly referred, and still less they apprehended of the horrors of the night which was then wrapping its mantle of darkness about the devoted islands. All but one.

Among these fisher-folk of Cheniere Caminada who noted the gathering storm was Andre Gilbeaux. Even while the sun was shining in the cloudless sky Gilbeaux sent out and summoned his relatives and friends to a banquet at sundown in his humble but happy home. They came, filled with anticipations 'of innocent enjoyment and gathered at the festal board.

The banquet was over, and, just as the sun sank beneath the waves the laughter and jest was stilled as the host rose to his feet with a glass of wine in his hand. At the sight of the expression on his face the smiles which had come to greet his expected toast died away, and a death-like silence fell upon all, leaving the ripple of the waters on the shelving shore and the rustling of the wind-waved marsh grass the only sounds.

Raising his glass, in a calm, collected voice he said:

"Gentlemen, this will be the last time we will be together, for to-night I will drown. There will be companions with me in my death. You may think that I am crazy, but I cannot help that, for I am firmly convinced that a watery death will be mine. I will now toast to all, and hope peace and rest will be mine. May God bless all that remain behind, and peace to my companions' ashes that will die with me."

Andre had always been a quiet, sober, self-contained man of evenly balanced mind and warm affections, a fond husband and a kind father. But now his friends thought his mind unbalanced, and his wife, the tears streaming from her eyes, implored his friend Seikard Gaspard (who survived to tell the tale) to dissuade her husband from the sin of self-destruction. Gilbeaux declared that suicide was far from his thoughts, but that others as well as himself would meet death in the waves, and he indicated who of those around the board would go with him into the valley of the shadow of death; and, strange as it may seem, he foretold correctly. Even as he spoke the dark clouds began to gather in the evening sky and moaning wind and heaving waters began to tell of the coming storm. The party scattered to their homes, and then the storm burst forth. Gilbeaux and his brother endeavored to save themselves and Gilbeaux's wife and children in a boat when the rising waters covered their island home. But Gilbeaux's prophecy was destined to be fulfilled. The boat was overturned and only Gilbeaux's brother lived to tell the tale.

Cheniere Caminada, often spoken of as an island, is really a peninsular, jutting into the waters of the Gulf of Mexico to the west of Grand Isle, and joined to the mainland by a marshy isthmus which is often covered by water. It is all sand and sea marsh and rises but a few feet above the gulf. There is no vegetation on it save a few stunted bushes, and its only inhabitants are the fishermen and their families.

Although less than a mile wide and but about two miles and a half long its population numbered on that fateful day 1471 souls.

A TYPICAL FISHERMAN'S HUT.

When the night came they retired to their homes, built, as described, on piles or "pickets" as they called them, and prepared for the day of toil they looked for on the morrow by seeking the repose that comes to him who labors for his bread. Parents

stilled the little ones who were terrified by the rising wind and
the waves, which were now dashing far beyond their accustomed limits and were washing with ever increasing fury
around the slender supports of the houses. But minute by
minute the storm increased. The wind blew stronger and
stronger until it swept across devoted Cheniere a hundred and
fifteen miles an hour; and the water, churned to a foam by the
merciless storm king, rolled across the whole peninsular in
towering waves which beat on the frail homes of thin board
and fragile latania like hammers of destruction. At last the
assaults of the elements began to tell upon these frail habitations, built only for such slight protection as was ordinarily
needed in that land of perennial summer.

A RUINED HOME AT CHENIERE.

Following the sweep of some wave mightier than its fellows,
or some blast which shrieked across the sedge grown morass
like a demon of destruction, would come a crash, which told of
the ruin of a happy home. Torn plank from plank by the wind
it was scattered in the inky darkness, or, beaten from its supporting piles by the angry sea, it disappeared in the raging
waters, and its occupants were face to face with death. For a
while the husband and father would make an unequal struggle with death for his loved ones, and then all would go
down in the storm lashed water. Again and again was this
scene repeated, and family after family, father, mother and
children, all, found eternal peace amid the warring of the elements, while their bodies were swept toward the marsh of the
mainland. Then came a lull and the inexperienced hoped
that the worst was over. But nature was but resting for a
mightier effort than she had yet put forth. Again came the
wind, this time from off the land; and again the waters swept
Cheniere. The debris of the homes previously wrecked, with
the huge trunks of trees torn from the earth on the shore

north of the Cheniere, battered down the dwellings which had withstood the first assault, while a ghastly procession of white faced corpses drifted by out to sea. When morning broke and the sun again looked down on the storm-swept strip of sand, it shown upon but five houses, all that was left of the five hundred that dotted the peninsular the evening before.

One of the few survivors was Pere Grimaux, the Roman Catholic priest of Cheniere Caminada. The account he gave a reporter of the destruction of his parish and the havoc in his flock was graphic and terrible The good priest said:

"The population of Cheniere Caminada island was 1471. Of these 696 only are now living; 779 are dead. Historic Cheniere Caminada is no more. The first effects of the storm were felt between 7 and 8 p. m. on Sunday. Everyone apprehended that something terrible was about to happen. The fishermen foreseeing that a serious storm was evident, hastened to beach their craft near their houses. But those precautions availed not, for the wind blew in fitful gusts, increasing in strength and velocity every minute, coming from the south. At 7:30 p. m. huge waves were madly lashing the shore, and in a few minutes they had attained a height of six feet, and later on of eight feet. There was one avenue of safety, and that was to seek the upper stories of the houses, but even that chance for escape was lost, when the wind and waves combined shook the frail habitations, which rocked to and fro and creaked and groaned under the repeated attacks of the furious elements. Soon the houses were being demolished, wrecked and carried away. The wind shifted to the southeast, and for hours shrieked with redoubled fury. Above the thundering voice of the hurricane could be heard the despairing cries, the groans and the frantic appeals for help of the unfortunate victims.

"I was in the upper story of the presbytery, holding on to the sill of an open window, powerless to do anything and exposed to the terrific blasts and hearing the cries of agony of my poor dying parishioners. A more furious attack of the storm broke off one-half of the roof. Notwithstanding the wind, I managed to light a lantern, which I displayed at the window, to serve as a beacon for those who might be fortunate enough to swim or to be cast towards the presbytery. Then I leaned forward and holding up my hands over the waste of waters, I offered a fervent prayer to the Father of all and beg-ged of him to be merciful in his judgment on the souls of so many of his children who were at that moment dying in such a sudden and terrible manner.

"I gave them all the final absolution of the Roman Catholic church.

"Then there was a sudden ominous lull in the storm. I felt that the worst was yet to come. It was then about 11 o'clock and I saw blacker and denser masses of clouds, swiftly rolling from the southeast towards our doomed island. There was something really appalling in that deceptive column. However, those few minutes of rest were precious and saved the lives of many people.

"Brave, sturdy men went out in skiffs and rowed from house to house, taking in such of the inhabitants as had escaped the first onslaught of the tempest. Many of these people sought shelter in two or three houses known to be solidly built, and this proved eventually their salvation, and in that way nearly 700 persons survived that fearful night.

FATHER GRIMEAUX.

"During the lull I looked out of the window and saw a young boy about 11 years old, clinging to a piece of timber and floating toward the presbytery. I called out to the men in the skiffs and told them to save that young life. But fate decreed otherwise. Just then the storm burst again with terrific violence and carried off the little fellow, to be seen no more. The wind had shifted and now blew from the west. Whatever of life and property had been spared by the south wind was destroyed by the gale from the west. Trees were snapped like reeds; houses were wrecked in an instant, and soon the Cheniere ceased to exist. Out of 450 houses only four remained, and these were filled with crowds of trembling, despairing people, bewailing not only their own sad, pitiful plight, but crying out the names of loved ones carried away by the merciless floods. All around and about me I could see desolation, death, ruin and wreck. Houses floated by and were seen no more. The church soon followed, I remained alone.

"As far as I could see there was not a vestige of any human habitation. Under my window the seething waters flowed madly on and I could see amidst the wreckage and the seaweed a number of bodies floating on and on out of view. I could not count them. It seemed to me like an endless, ghastly, horrible procession of spectres. Unable to bear that terrible sight any more, I closed my eyes and leaning my forehead on my hand, realized that everything was inextricably lost. I never dreamed that I would live through that horrible ordeal.

"Again I heard those heart-rending cries. Looking on by a strong effort of will power, I saw floating past women and children, some of the women holding in their arms their infants, while some of those unfortunate young ones were tightly grasping the dresses of their mothers. Not a few were clutching even the arms and tresses of the women. Ever and anon one of the little victims, apparently worn out, would release his hold and be quickly carried away by the raging waters after a last frantic adieu.

"A large number of people were saved by holding on to floating debris, such as parts of roofs, timbers, etc. Some of them were considerably bruised and injured, but their lives were spared, and when morning dawned and the storm had somewhat abated, they painfully found their way to houses in which their relatives and friends had found refuge during that eventful night.

"A young boy named Cyriac Prosperi was found on these a shore two days and one night after the storm. He was deprived of his clothing by the storm. His only sustenance was an orange that had drifted in his way.

"On Monday about 3 a. m. the storm was over. My sister and myself knelt down and thanked the sacred heart of Jesus and Our Lady of Good Help for our safety. We had invoked them in our hour of peril and to them we owed our deliverance. At day break three men came to the presbytery and gave us a ladder to enable us to descend. Then a weary walk began. We waded in water waist deep, our feet sinking into the soil, thus adding to our discomfort and thus impeding our progress. We were on our way to succor the unfortunate people. Not a word was spoken; we looked at each other; we understood what was to be done; tears welled up to our eyes as we went along beholding new and untold miseries at every step.

"Monday and Tuesday we hardly rested, being occupied in burying the dead. More than 400 corpses were unburied. Many could not be found for they had been carried out to the gulf. On Tuesday, more affliction. We began to feel the want of fresh water: then we realized also that we had no provisions. The excitement and the exertion in giving burial to the hundreds of dead people had made us forgetful of our own physical wants. Now we felt exhausted and at night we were completely prostrated. The odor emanating from the dead bodies, both of man and beast, made the situation all the more unbearable.

"The arrival of two boats laden with ice was hailed with joy. We lost no time in melting the ice and mixing it with a small proportion of salt water so as to increase the quantity. Other boats came from the city with provisions donated by the charitable people of New Orleans.

"This relief was timely, for we had saved nothing at all from the destructive storm.

"Houses had been swept away, luggers, schooners, boats of all description had been lost. We could only lay claim to a few tattered bits of clothing.

"The people of Cheniere and Grand Isle fervently hope and trust that the kind-hearted people of this State will hasten to send them the relief that is so imperatively and immediately needed.

"Most of the inhabitants of the Cheniere are very poor people, fishermen, whose only worldly possessions were their huts and their boats. These they have lost and how will they be able to earn their living? Who will come to their aid and help them to rebuild their humble abodes?"

This was no overdrawn picture, as was seen by the rescuing parties which went from New Orleans when the tale of destruction reached that city two days later, and whose work will be told later on. On Monday the few survivors, worn out by their long and terrible battle for life, found and buried one hundred and fifty bodies; and then exhausted nature gave out, the efforts to render the last duty to the dead ceased, and they threw themselves on the bare sands to wait the rescue they hardly dared hope for, or the death which now stared them in the face in another form. The salt waves which had covered the Cheniere had swept to sea every mouthful of food and every drop of fresh water; for these people had neither wells nor springs, and drank only rain water caught and stored in cask-like cisterns of staves and hoops, which stood above ground. Six hundred human beings, men, women and children, on this strip of sand, cut off from the mainland by impassable marshes, with their boats destroyed and the nearest help over fifty miles away as the crow flies, near a hundred by the bayous, the only avenue of communication, and no means of making their plight known! Can the human imagination picture a condition more terrible? For twenty-four awful hours no help arrived. Then a lugger which had gone to New Orleans before the storm for ice, with which these fishermen preserved their catch, returned. This ice was the salvation of the people who had escaped the fury of the tempest. It was quickly melted, and mixed with sea water to increase its quantity, it was nectar to the thirst-tormented survivors. Then came twenty-four hours more of suffering before help came from the city. Revived by the water, the living began again to bury the dead. This had to be done in the most primitive manner. There was no lumber to make coffins, and neither nails nor tools to use, had there been lumber; there were not even implements with which to dig the graves. Long trenches were scooped in the sand with broken boards and sticks and even with the bare hands of the toilers, and ten, fifteen, twenty, even thirty bodies were laid in the same grave, with only mother earth for their winding sheet and the gently lapping waters of the gulf for their funeral service.

One of the mostly ghastly scenes after the flood was the little cemetery. The ruthless water had respected "God's Acre" no more than it did the possessions of man, and the resting places of the dead were shattered as were the dwellings of the living. Tombs were rent asunder, graves were torn open, crosses and monuments and headstones were destroyed. Even the crumbling bones of the dead were torn from their resting places and scattered over the sites of the ruined homes of their descendants. Great trunks of trees, foul smelling seaweed, timbers torn from the houses and the flotsom and jetsam of the surging waters were strewn in tangled chaos "where the rude forefathers of the hamlet slept." But the people of Cheniere, the few survivors, were unable to bury the victims of the storm, much less to repair the last resting places of their older dead; and when the rescuing parties arrived from New Orleans they had all they could do in caring for the famishing remnant, in binding up the wounds of the injured, and in searching on the sands of the beach, in the long grass of the marshes, among the slimy recesses of the dismal swamps, under the torn and shattered cypress and oaks, with their funeral drapery of sombre moss, for the bodies of the newly dead.

THE WRECKED CEMETERY AT CHENIERE.

CHAPTER II.

GRAND ISLE.

When the present century was young there was one name which was spoken in the lowlands of South Louisiana, along the sun-kissed sands of its southern shore, on the waters of the Gulf of Mexico, with bated breath. It was the name of Jean Marie Lafitte, the pirate of the gulf. Originally a blacksmith in New

"I AM THE ONLY ONE LEFT."

Orleans, he became the agent of the privateers commissioned by the United States of Columbia in the struggle with Spain for independence. From agent to active participant was but a short step for Lafitte, and the step from privateer to pirate was shorter still. Lafitte's knowledge of the country stood the band in good stead. A short distance below New Orleans the country through which the Mississippi river flows begins to contract, and soon it becomes a narrow finger of firm land running out into the gulf, the river flowing on along its middle, while its outer edges are at first bounded by flat sea marsh, soon giving place to the waters of the gulf which sweep up on both sides to within a few hundred yards of the river bank in two bold crescents whose horns meet at the point where the father of waters pours his mighty floods into the sea.

This marsh country is threaded by tortuous bayous which have their sources near the river just below New Orleans, and some of them debouche from the river itself. Gradually they draw themselves away from the parent stream, and, striking through the swamp, their sluggish currents seek the gulf to the west of the mouth of the Mississippi.

For a time they flow along with current so sluggish and between banks so even and so equidistant at different points that they would be taken for artificial canals were it not for their winding course.

Chief among these many waterways is Bayou Barataria. It winds in and out, through fertile fields and dank swamps, now glittering like a silver ribbon in the sun which strikes it over the verdant billows of waving cane, now sullenly gleaming like a river of ink in the shadows of the moss hung oaks and cypress whose branches arch its tortuous channel. For miles it runs a narrow canal seeming scarce wide enough for the tiny steamer which beats its waters with its single wheel, or the solitary lugger which is the ordinary carrier of its primitive commerce; then it breaks into a lake resting like a hugh pearl on the bosom of a prairie; then contracting again to its normal width it glides by a "settlement" perched on its banks, again to become a lake which glistens in the sunlight like an immense dew drop caught in the dense undergrowth of an impenetrable swamp. Now it sweeps through a sea marsh over which comes the salt-laden breeze fresh from its caressing of the ocean; now it gently touches the edges of a "trembling prairie," (that queer formation of a shell of earth in the bosom of an unfathomable depth of water, whose grassy surface undulates like the sea) as if it too feared that treacherous land which has often given way beneath the feet of the venturesome hunter and made its hidden waters his unknown tomb. At last, weary of its wanderings, it meets the salt water of the gulf in Barataria bay. Lying at the mouth of Barataria bay where it joins the Gulf of Mexico are the twin islands of Grand Isle and Grande Terre. Their oaks and undergrowth afforded a shelter for the freebooters of the deep, their shallow waters, with channels known only to their constant frequenters, gave a security to the pirate schooners from chase and capture by the deep draft war vessels, and Bayou Barataria afforded an easy means of conveying spoil to secret agents in the City of New Orleans. All this was well known to Jean Lafitte, and when put in command he selected Grand Isle as his headquarters. Here he built store-houses and sheds, and here he erected what was known as "the pirate's house," until the storm of October 1, 1893, swept the last vestige of it from the earth. But years before that date it had been put to more peaceful use, and sheltered there those who were content with the spoils taken from the sea by honest toil, instead of that garnered under the shadow of the black flag.

With the passing away of the pirate crew, the fame of Grand Isle for balmy breezes, and safe surf bathing spread abroad. Soon a few summer cottages made their appearance among the homes of the fishermen; then others followed; then hotels were built, and, finally, when the busy weavers at the loom of commerce stretched one of their steel threads from the Crescent

LAFITTE'S OLD HOUSE AT GRAND ISLE.

City toward Barataria Bay and began to hurl backward and forward the iron shuttle which weaves the web of our prosperity, the Ocean Club Hotel reared its pretentious form among its humbler neighbors, with room for a thousand guests; and summer after summer the gilded butterflies of fashion flocked from the city to spend the heated term in this romantic spot.

Fortunately most of the summer guests had left Grand Isle before the great storm, and this alone is the reason why the mortality there did not nearly approach that at ill-fated Cheniere Caminada. ℱ Had the storm occurred a month earlier, its consequences would have been appalling; for when the large summer hotels were wrecked by the winds and their timbers tossed about by the angry waters, had they been filled, as they were during August and September, with women and children, those who would have escaped could have been counted on the fingers.

Another thing in favor of Grand Isle is the difference between its formation and that of Cheniere. The last is a mere sand spit, formed by the action of the waves, while Grand Isle rests on a rock foundation and is formed of shell deposits, drift-wood, sand and the washings from alluvial Louisiana. And while the whole of Cheniere Caminada lay open to the sweep of the waves, Grand Isle, on the south, is protected from the gulf by a range of low sand hills, thrown up by the sea, which acted as a breakwater when the hurricane seemed to hurl the gulf on human beings crouched in terror on its shore.

When the storm struck Grand Isle on that terrible Sunday night there were about three hundred people on the island, most of them permanent residents. Of these only some twenty-eight or thirty were killed, but many were badly injured and all suffered severely for food and water before the arrival of the relief boats. They retire early at Grand Isle, and when the tempest came nearly all the inhabitants were in bed and many were asleep. Two sailors, Ertivez and Mergovich, who were up and out of doors gave a graphic description of the scene. They said the wind had been rather high in the afternoon and increased to a gale when night fell. About ten o'clock they went out of the house. The storm was then seemingly at its height and they became afraid the island would be overwhelmed, and they determined to try and escape in a boat to the mainland. They ran to a cove where the boat was beached and worked amid the roar of tempest, the crash of falling trees and shattered houses and the thundering of the water on the shore, to launch their frail craft. Then, said they, there came a lull. For an instant that seemed like an age, there was perfect quiet, and then the warring of the elements began again with redoubled force. The wind had chopped around and now blew in almost a directly opposite direction from its former course. The first blow had forced the waters in from the gulf and had set a strong current in shore. The second blow forced back this water and with it that of the bay and the bayous behind the islands, and started a counter current running out to sea. When these two mighty masses of water met in the gulf off shore a wave was created whose foam decked crest towered thirty feet in the air, and which rushed upon the devoted island.

By the flash of the lightning which illumined the inky darkness these sailors saw this tidal wave sweeping down like the besom of destruction. What could puny human might do? The sand hills which had been counted upon as a protection were no more than so many straws in the path of this awful wave. It tore them as the incoming tide destroys the sand piles the children build in their play. It swept over them as if they had been

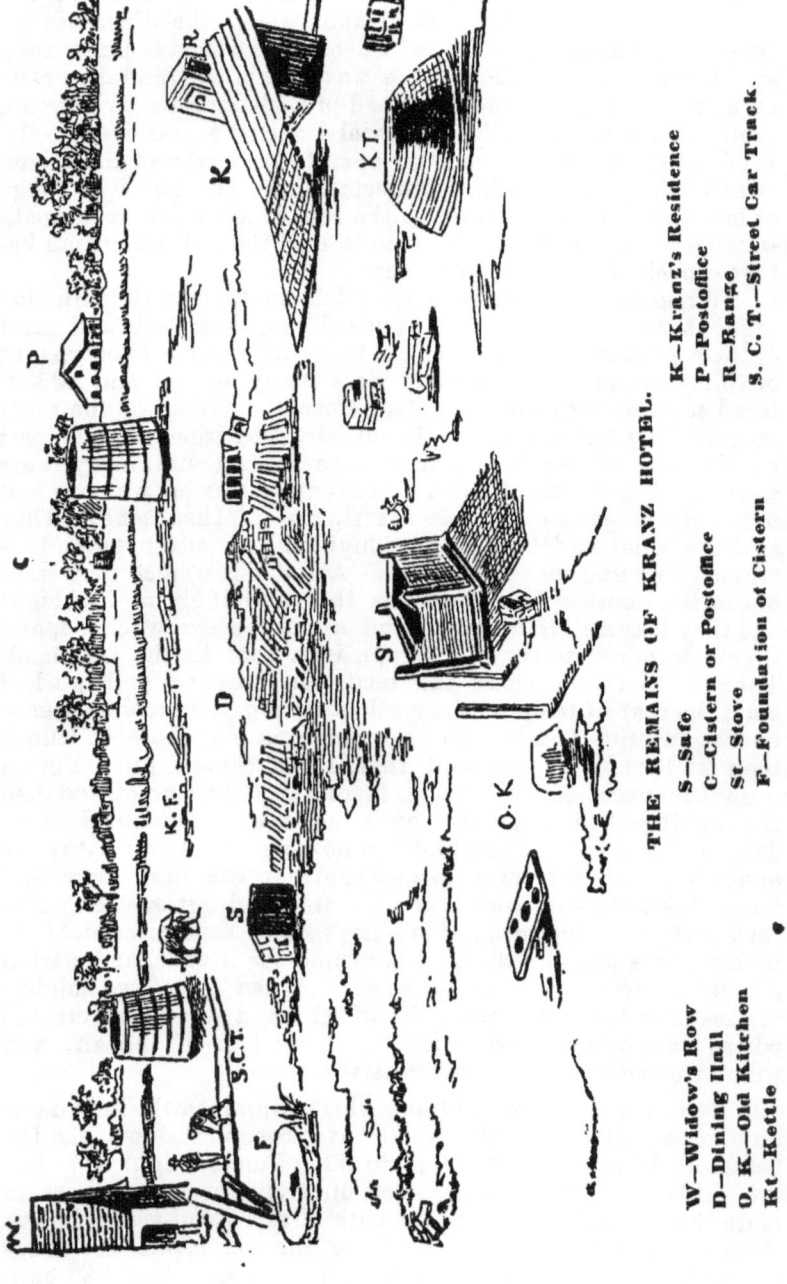

THE REMAINS OF KRANZ HOTEL.

W—Widow's Row
D—Dining Hall
O. K.—Old Kitchen
Kt—Kettle

S—Safe
C—Cistern or Postoffice
St—Stove
F—Foundation of Cistern

K—Kranz's Residence
P—Postoffice
R—Range
S. C. T.—Street Car Track.

but ripples in the sand left by a retiring tide and rushed to complete the work of destruction the wind had commenced. The island was engulfed. Houses were washed away, cattle were drowned, trees were torn from the ground and tossed like straws in its boiling surface. The railroad track leading from one of the hotels down to the beach was utterly destroyed: the ties were torn from the ground and splintered as if by axes in the hands of a thousand woodmen; the rails were wrenched apart and, borne like corks by the angry waters, and tossed hundreds of yards away, some of them wrapped and twined around trees, as if some mighty Vulcan had done it in sportive derision of his human imitators.

Krantz's Hotel, a collection of cottages with a large assembly hall and dining room at either end, was utterly destroyed, and Captain Krantz, the proprietor, severely injured, his life being saved by the exertions of a servant.

The Ocean Club Hotel, a large three story structure, built with a special view of resisting storms, with its planking doubled and spiked on at right angles, and the whole building buttressed with three large Ls, was wrecked. The upper story was swept away and utterly destroyed, while the two lower ones were twisted and torn out of all semblance of a house. Windows and doors were beaten in, great gaps were torn in the walls and wreckage and seaweed and dead bodies of animals were piled in and over it. The house built by Jean Lafitte, a strong substantial cottage on brick pillars, and occupied as a dwelling, was utterly destroyed; not a stick of its timbers was left on its site; even the foundation was torn to pieces, and only a few scattered bricks were left to mark the spot where once it stood. The house where he had lived and the shop where he had worked in New Orleans had long before fallen before the march of improvement, and now the storm had erased the last trace left in Louisiana of the pirate of the gulf.

Captain Krantz gave to a reporter of the New Orleans Picayune the following graphic account of the storm:

"I am 70 years old, and for many years have owned the Grand Isle Hotel. I am a widower with four children. On the night of the storm I was at home. I did not expect that anything serious would happen. The wind rose about 9 o'clock and blew hard. At 11 o'clock it changed and blew from the varying points from northwest to southwest at intervals of fifteen minutes thereafter. In about half an hour the water on the grounds around the hotel was fully five feet deep. A terrible gust of wind struck the house and knocked it over. A portion of the building fell on me, and for a time I thought our last hour had come.' Fortunately the water continued to rise, and in about ten minutes I felt the weight pressing heavily upon my body gradually removed. I was lying on a beam. I was washed away from under the house, the water carrying me with it for a distance of twenty-five feet. I was struck and became unconscious. For several hours I did not know what had occurred to me. When I regained consciousness it was 5 o'clock on Sunday morning. I was still clinging to the beam, which was firmly embedded in the ground opposite my bathhouse. I received very serious injuries. In my feeble condition I returned to what had been the hotel, but out of the thirty-eight cottages which formerly stood there only twenty were left. There was not a particle of food to be found, everything having been washed away, including all the wearing apparel. I estimate my loss at from $75,000 to $100,000."

The first boat which went to the relief of the sufferers carried the son of the old captain to his father's rescue. The relief boat met one of the few luggars left by the storm on its way to New Orleans for help, and Captain Krantz was on board. The meeting between father and son was most affecting. The injured veteran was brought aboard the steamer and made as comfortable as possible, and with careful nursing was finally restored to health.

One of the most thrilling experiences at Grand Isle on that night of horrors was that of the crew of the little steamer Joe Webre, the boat that has for many years travelled back and forth between New Orleans and Grand Isle, carrying the crowds that sought the beautiful island resort in winter and summer. Many a storm she safely weathered, but at last she went to pieces and only her name remains to remind many of happy trips down the bayous and across the little lakes, that dot the course between New Orleans and Grand Isle. When the wind became dangerously strong, extra ropes were put out, and eight inch and a quarter cables were hove about the piles of Grand Isle pier where the storm overtook the boat. To relieve the terrific strain on the cables, a full head of steam was turned on, and everyone on the boat stood ready for the worst when it came. The skies grew blacker, and the waves rose higher and higher, their crests lashed to white foam, and in the depths between, the phosphorescent gleaming of the churned water caused the boat to seem about to plunge in an abyss of fire when she started down from the top of a huge wave. The cables parted and the Webre drifted out into the gulf at the mercy of the wind. Debris from ruined Cheniere Caminada and Grand Isle drifted by her and dashed against her sides. When the wind lulled for a few moments, the cries of wounded and dying came from the distant islands and added to the horror of the night. Then the Webre trembled from stanchion to keel, and the cabin was blown to pieces. The crew, Captain McSweeney, George Rolf, engineer; Pilot Pegreagan, Richard, pantryman; Albert Foster, cook; Elizabeth Lyle, chambermaid, and Charley Green, deck hand, all gathered on deck and together left the boat in a yawl when they saw she was sure to go to pieces. Just as they pulled out from the boat a lull came—a dead calm fell upon the waters and not even the smallest zephyr ruffled the waves. But the quiet that came so suddenly seemed ominous, and all expected what followed—a renewal of the storm with tenfold fury. But the wind had shifted and now came from off the island. Each gust was fiercer than the last and the crew saw the Webre go down, while their skiff was overturned and dashed to pieces. Fortunately the crew were beside a tree that had withstood the assault of wind and waves, and they took refuge in its branches.

The chambermaid was a negro woman who weighed nearly 300, and it may be easier imagined than described how she was hauled up in the tree and held there while the gale blew with terrific force. George Rolfs, Jr., the brave engineer, tells the following story:

THE WRECK OF THE JOE WEBRE.

"I will never forget my experience. We were all on board of the boat when the storm arose. Steam was up and we were preparing to go. The wind increased to such an extent that we were obliged in order to keep our feet to hold on to the hog chains. The boat was striking the wharf with such power that it became difficult for us to stir. The hogchain parted speedily under the strain, and then we took refuge beside the ice box. A wave swept the deck and soon carried the latter protection from us. The wind then suddenly calmed, and we took shelter in the pilot house. Soon we had to leave that spot. Our next attempt to find a place of safety caused us nearly to be washed overboard. The boat was becoming a wreck, she having parted from her moorings. We launched the yawlboat and rowed through the darkness for the Grand Isle Hotel. After pulling hard for some time, we reached the place where the buildings were supposed to be located, and were surprised to find nothing but a continuous sheet of turbulent water. The entire party climbed an oak tree and remained there till daylight when we descended. The water had then abated considerably, and was not more than two feet deep. We walked to an old shanty, where we found refuge for several hours. We finally left there in search of Captain Krantz. In our search we visited a house in which there was an old lady, a woman and a young girl, where we remained until the water had entirely disappeared. Word having reached us that Captain Krantz was alive and not very seriously injured, we returned to the wharf. Here we found that the Joe Webre had been blown back and was high and dry on the ground. She was a total wreck. She had broken clean in half."

The boat was lifted from her place in front of Grand Isle by the wind when it veered, and she was carried 250 feet inland, and now lies across the railroad track built by Captain Kranz to carry guests from the hotel to the bay, high and dry, a complete wreck.

) Geo. Rolfs, Jr., the engineer of the wrecked steamer, Joe Webre, has a memento of the storm in the shape of his gold watch, which he wore until the beating rain drenched his clothing, and he took it off and placed it under his pillow in his stateroom, where, a few moments later, the fireman also placed his watch, both men supposing by so doing they would save their time pieces from a soaking. But the vessel went to pieces, and the cabin was blown away, and its remnants were scattered far and wide over the waters, and in that hour of peril, when the crew left the boat, expecting to find watery graves, neither Mr. Rolfs nor the fireman gave a thought to their watches. Afterward, when they were rescued, they exchanged mutual condolence at the loss of their timepieces, never expecting to see them again, as they knew the cabin of the Webre had been blown to pieces and carried to sea. But when Mr. Geo. Rolfs, father was sent to examine the hulk of the wrecked Webre, ten days later, he saw something gleaming among the sand and dirt in the hull, and to his amazement brought to light his son's watch, when he dug up the shining metal from its bed of mud. Where its companion, the fireman's timepiece is, cannot be conjectured, but Mr. Rolfs prizes his water-soaked watch far more than he did when it ticked regularly and told him the time for starting his boat on her trips.

)Just to the east of Grand Isle lies Grande Terre, also an island. Here the storm was equally severe, but no lives were lost, owing, no doubt, to the fact that but few persons were there, and these few took refuge in the fort built there by the United States government on the west end of the island to guard the channel which passes between Grande Terre and Grand Isle into Barataria bay. But as solid as was this massive work it could not withstand the furious assaults of the ocean. For a while the sturdy fortification repulsed the attacks of the waves as they thundered up the beach against its grassy sides. But at last a breach was made; the works of man could not stand forever before the irresistible assaults of nature in her might. The angle of the fort next the gulf was torn off and the waves, following each other like the successive lines of an assaulting army, entered the works. They wrought still further destruction on slope and glacis, in casemate and on rampart; but those who had entered the fort for safety retired to the part which the waters spared, and all escaped. Here, as elsewhere, houses were leveled, trees were torn from the earth, animals were killed by the storm and drowned in the rising waters, property was destroyed and men were beggared, but Grande Terre was one of the few spots where was not heard the wailing of the saved for the untimely dead.

CHAPTER III.

ON THE MISSISSIPPI.

The storm did not confine itself to the islands of Barataria Bay alone, nor even to the coast line of the gulf. Its ravages were felt far up the Mississippi river. Nor were those ravages felt alone along the narrow tongue of land through which the river flows for the last few miles of its length, as has been described heretofore, but they were manifest far inland where the wind and water from the gulf had to sweep over a wide stretch of country to reach the banks of the father of waters. A few miles below New Orleans the settled and cultivated country begins to "contract" and it grows narrower and narrower until just above forts Jackson and St. Philip it ceases altogether and the river sweeps from there to sea between marshy banks, with only here and there the hut of a fisherman, or other person who draws his living from the water, to break the monotony of the view. There is one exception, and that is the group of buildings which compose the Louisiana Quarantine Station—the post where stand the sentinels who guard the Mississippi Valley from invasion by contagious and infectious diseases. These buildings include the large fumigating house, the boat house and telegraph station, the storehouse and the quarters for the physicians and employees who are always stationed there. And laying at the wharf, or sheltered in the boat house are the fumigating tug boat, the steam launch and the numerous row boats, large and small, with which the station is equipped.

From the quarantine station to the gulf the river banks are duplicates of what they are above, except where the hand of man has changed them for his purposes. At the "head of the passes," where the river spreads itself like the fingers of an opened hand, and seeks the gulf by three different channels, commence the Eads' Jetties, those mighty works which have harnessed the theretofore wasted power of the resistless river and made it dig its own bed and deepen its own channel. To the one who sees them for the first time they are disappointing, for there is little to show for the money which has been spent and the results which have been accomplished. But these great works are chiefly beneath the water, with only the heads of the piles and a few stones showing above the surface. But as you approach the gulf the jetties show more and more until the "sea-wall," built of great blocks of granite, give evidence that man has indeed been here at work.

At the very mouth of the river, perched between the river and the gulf, is Port Eads. Here is the first boarding station of the quarantine, and here also are the homes of the pilots who take in and out of the river the ocean carriers who make New Orleans their port. How these places were served by the storm will be told at the proper time in this story; the intention now is to try and give the reader some idea of the river, or at least that part of it which suffered on the night of Sunday, October 1, 1893. The first point below New Orleans where the storm commenced to do its work of destruction was the old "Poydras" plantation. From there down, Stella, Monsecour, Old Harlem, Myrtle Grove, Savoy, Belleview, Hebert's, Livaudais, Sardelot's, in short, all of the plantations suffered more or less from the storm. Houses were unroofed or blown down, fences were leveled, the crops of cane and rice were badly injured, animals were killed or drowned, and sugar houses were badly damaged by the wind and water; but, fortunately no lives were lost.

At Point Celeste a large negro church was torn from its foundations by the storm, carried over a quarter of a mile and deposited squarely across the track of the New Orleans, Fort Jackson and Grand Isle Railroad.

At Tropical Bend occurred the first loss of life on the river. Here several colored people lost their lives, some from drowning, but most from flying timbers. Near here occurred the pathetic death of Mrs. Lafrance, which is related elsewhere.

The only town of any size on the Mississippi river below New Orleans is Pointe-a-la-Hache, the seat of justice of Plaquemines parish. The ravages of the storm here were frightful. Nearly every house in the little town was badly damaged;

AIDING COLORED SUFFERERS.

many of them were blown down. Its three churches were
unroofed, their windows were destroyed, their doors blown in,
and they were deluged with water. The jail was unroofed,
and the courthouse, just finished at a cost of $16,000, was badly
injured; the slates were torn from the roof, the doors and windows were smashed and the massive clock tower with its costly
clock, was thrown to the ground a mass of broken bricks. As
the demon of the storm shrieked through the place, the air
was filled with flying debris; bricks and timbers were hurled
through the air as if they had been feathers and straw. The
terrified inhabitants knew not what to do; the crashing of
houses warned them that death lurked for them in the dwellings that sheltered them, while the missles of destruction
which hurtled through the darkness of the night without were
almost certain death to anyone who sought to escape in the
open air.

The family of Mr. Mandots met with serious injuries. The
family was huddled up in the house when the tornado struck
it, and in less time than it takes to tell, the force of the wind
had splintered the rafters and blown the house down on top
of the unfortunates who had trusted to its security.

The ferry-boat at Pointe-a-la-Hache was caught by the
gale, and before a rope could be started or another line secured, the ferry was smashed into kindling wood. Two luggers, which were hugging the shore to avoid the fury of the
gale, were caught as the tornado swerved and they also shared
the general fate.

Throughout the time of the gale the rain fell in a perfect
sheet. The drops were large, and the violence of the wind
was so great as to give one subjected to the rain the sensation
of being assailed by a million peas hurled with mighty force.

A sample of the force and fury of the wind was seen in the
condition of two cars of the New Orleans, Fort Jackson and
Grand Isle road at this point. They had been standing on
the track at the station hitched to other cars of the train, and
the big wind that swept the town picked them up completely
from the earth, breaking the coupling pin that connected them
with the other cars of the train and turning them over. The
escape of the two men inside was nothing short of miraculous.
The cars were jammed into the soft mud alongside the railroad and the windows and cornice work were smashed to
pieces. The heavy iron truck work underneath was torn
asunder as though it had been so much thread.

A reporter of the New Orleans Picayune thus described
the scene in and around the newspaper office in Pointe-a-la-
Hache next day:

"The first place to attract attention was the little printing
office of the Plaquemines Protector, the newspaper of the par-

ish, edited by Robert E. Hingle. Mr. Hingle is one example of the indomitable spirit of the newspaper man. His office and print shop is a small frame structure, standing out on the road, and it bears the resemblance of having been on a protracted drunk. In shipping parlance, it is on its beam ends, and is kept from collapsing by two or three braces. All the type and everything else in the structure, was "pied"—heaped about in indescribable confusion. He managed to save one form with the type locked in it, partially intact, and this, with with the aid of an assistant, he has distributed in a battered case, set up in a room adjoining the store, and despite the work of the elements he will issue his paper as usual, though in a necessarily abbreviated form.

"The home of his nephew, a neat frame cottage was blown to pieces, and some of the pieces of timber hurled about with such force that they stuck in the ground 10 feet deep. The escape of the family was miraculous. The high wind in the early part of the night warned them to be on the lookout, and as the storm grew in intensity their alarm increased, for the creaking of the timbers in the house told them it was unsafe. A falling cornice decided them to leave it, and no sooner had they gone when it collapsed with a crash. Not a member of his family or his nephew's family sustained the slightest injury, other reports, to the contrary, notwithstanding.

"A short distance further on a sad sight was presented. There stood what had but two days before been a handsome, roomy house, with nothing but the gaunt, bare weather-beaten walls standing and the roof and chimney scattered in all directions. In the rear the kitchen, evidently a more substantial structure, stood comparatively intact, and here the family of Maurice Maurin were huddled. The bedding and clothing of the family were hanging on clothes lines, and the projecting portions of the battered house, drying, for the rain had thoroughly wet everything in the house and kitchen. None of the people were injured, as they left the tottering building just before it fell. The stable in the rear dropped as if a heavy weight had crushed it flat down; only the roof was perfectly intact."

These scenes could be repeated over and over again, but enough has been given to convey some idea of the destruction at this point.

Bohemia is a little hamlet on the river below Pointe-a-la-Hache, and is the temporary terminus of the railroad. This is a little village comprising fifty or more negroes, who live in small wooden cabins. This is Dr. Herbert's rice plantation, and is about five miles below Pointe-a-la-Hache. The cabins, numbering probably twenty, are in a double row, facing a roadway which runs from the levee back to the rear. The greatest violence of the storm seemed to have been exerted on the row on the north side of the road. The first cabin was apparently intact, but its roof was damaged to such an extent that it is really uninhabitable. The next was more than half demolished, and bedding and cooking utensils and other household goods were scattered in utmost confusion over the debris. Of the third cabin naught remained but the flooring and the foundations, and the same may be said of all the rest in this part of the village.

Bedding and clothing were scattered everywhere, and the former residents seemed not to have made any efforts to secure their property, or rather what was left of it. At the end of the row there was a boarding-house, a structure of fair size, altogether of wood. The bare floor is all that is left, and standing up in the center, in seeming mockery of the work of the elements, was a sewing machine, which seemed to be still in perfect condition.

Of the houses on the south row, every one had rough board porticoes. These porticoes had all been broken off at their junction with the body of the house and forced down like the cover of a book over the doors and windows. At the end of the roadway there had formerly been an old wooden sugarhouse. It had been a commodious structure, but no longer served its original purpose, and had been for a long time used as a storehouse for grain and threshing machines. It was piled up in a tangled heap. The threshing machines were badly damaged, as well as the other contents of the building.

On the north side of the roadway there had also been a large structure used as a stable. This collapsed, and over twenty-five head of cattle, which were in it, were killed.

Only one person was injured here, and she was a woman, who was only slightly hurt.

The 80-foot carsheds at Bohemia were seen lying flat or heaped on top of some freight cars. There is a wharf there, where it was expected that steamers would land, but not many ever stop there. Two freight cars were lying half over on their sides, and beyond the wharf the water had run over the levee and washed it badly.

Two hundred feet from this spot was a heap of debris—the remnant of the cabin occupied by Charlotte Koinkel, a negress. She was a young woman, and had but recently rented the place which fell upon her and crushed her life out in an instant.

The Grand Prairie extends for a great distance below Bohemia, and also comprises what is known as the Union settlement. This place contains about 100 inhabitants, not more, and but three cabins were left standing Four casualties occurred here. The names of the dead are· Wily Anderson, a son of John Perrot, a daughter of Henry Johnson, one unknown man. All these were colored.

From here on down to the Quarantine Station it was the same story—destruction of life and property—over and over again, and to repeat it would be but to harrow up the feelings of the reader.

On Magnolia plantation (Gov. Warmoth's) the wreck was terrible. Many buildings had been unroofed and some of the houses had been wholly wrecked. The sugarhouse had been partially unroofed and while the orange trees had weathered the storm pretty well, the ground was literally covered with well matured fruit. The immense cane field which was one of the finest in the State had been blown flat, a considerable portion having been literally blown out of the ground.

A WRECKED INTERIOR.

This was one of the finest plantations in the State, and the orange grove was the finest in the South. The damage here was not less than $25,000, but the ex-governor bore his losses like a stoic—the only remark he made being "Thank God, none of my people were killed."

The magnificent quarantine station of the State of Louisiana, described at the beginning of this chapter, suffered severely. The medical staff at the station anticipated a storm, but not a destructive one like that which visited the place. Sunday night the Quarantine tugboat Aspinwall, with Captain John Roig, Engineer James O'Neill, and a manly crew, was lying near the quarantine wharf. The boat had steam up, and was waiting for

the heavy winds to abate some, so as to make a trip to one of
the steamers, for the purpose of disinfecting and fumigating it.
She had been on the leeward shore, and was just moving out
when the storm began in all its fury, and the tug was blown on
the batture. The jar was a terrible one, and as the boat plowed on
the batture the greater portion of the upper works was torn off.
The crew were thrown forcibly on their faces, and they began at
once to try and escape from the almost wrecked boat. Then
began a struggle to get ashore, and after running the greatest of
risks of life and limb they reached there safely, but badly shaken
up and frightened from their terrible experience. There were
men in the messroom, and the wind blew with such velocity that
every moment the men thought their place of shelter would be
blown down and all lost. They tried to escape, and after a difficult struggle in the wind and blinding rain they reached the
shed where the iron heating cylinders are, and crawled in the
cylinders for safety. These cylinders are made of boiler iron,
and are about fifty feet long and six feet in diameter. They are
three in number and into them all textile fabrics from suspected
vessels are put and are subjected to a treatment by dry heat and
moist heat, the cylinders being hermetically sealed. These
structures proved arks of safety for the men at the station while
the work of destruction was going on outside.

The plank walks were blown away, and it was at the
greatest risk for one to try and leave the place where he was
for safer quarters. The weather-boarding of the boathouse
was torn away, and the physician's launch was wrecked, with
a few big skiffs. The big roof over the disinfecting shed was
blown almost completely off, only a small portion remaining.
All along the course of the wind, trees and crops were destroyed, and a few small cabins were blown down, but there
was no one reported as being hurt or killed.

The Charles Chamberlin, a towboat belonging to the
Ocean Towboat Company, was lying along side a barkentine
when the storm came up, and to seek the harbor and tie up, the
boat left the barkentine and tried to make the dangerous trip.
The wind tossed her on the big swelling waves and with great
force sent her into a rice field, so that she could not get off.
No one was hurt and a portion of her crew was sent in a row-
boat to the Quarantine station and asked that the Aspinwall
be sent to the imperilled boat's assistance, but that tug was
also in need of assistance. The Aspinwall was damaged to
the extent of about $3500, while the Chamberlin was probably
damaged to the extent of a few hundred dollars. There were
other trifling damages done to a few smaller boats, but not to
any great extent. Fortunately here there was no loss of life.

At the Jetties, where the yellow flood of the mighty Mississippi plunges into the green waters of the gulf, the storm

raged furiously; the wind shrieked across the narrow tongue
of land like a thousand demons. The gauge showed that its
velocity exceeded one hundred miles an hour. The driving
rain was hurled by the wind until it stung like red hot shot.
The veterans among the bar pilots, those old salts who have
spent their lives battling with the elements, declared that
nothing in their experience had ever equalled it. Everything
loose was picked up and hurled far out to sea; the jetties
were stripped bare of everything movable in the twinkling of
an eye. But things there were built for blows, and but little
damage was done. As the gale increased the long, steady
swell of the gulf increased until at last the towering waves
thundered against the sea wall and, making a clean breach
over wall and jetties and land, they rolled to join the salt
water on the other side of the delta. The people on the west
shore took refuge in the lighthouse, which stood like a rock,
its beacon light shining out over the raging waters like the
star of hope; the people on the east bank gathered in the
small hotel which rocked like a ship in the gale, but which
weathered the storm in safety. There was one death here.
James Casey, the watchman for the jetty company, went out
to see if he could do anything for the safety of the property
committed to his care. He was begged not to go, but he an-
swered "It's my duty," and out into the storm he went. He
had gone but a short distance along the narrow jetty when
the wind lifted him from his feet and hurled him far out into
the raging waters. He battled bravely for his life, and his
cries for help could be heard above the howling of the storm.
But no boat could live an instant in those seething waters, nor
was there a boat left, all had been swept away; and so brave
Jim Casey went down to death, a martyr to duty.

While the storm was raging the worst, when the wind was
shrieking as if all the fiends of pandemonium were unchained,
and the rain drove in horizontal sheets, the people crouching
terrified in the lighthouse and hotel were dumbfounded to hear
the hoarse notes of a steamship's whistle. It did not seem possible that any ship made by mortal hands could live in that terrific tempest, and a few of the hardiest spirits ventured to look
out, not knowing whether or not they would see some spectre
ship or demon steamer ploughing through the air. To their as-
tonishment, almost horror, they saw the dark form and flashing
lights of an ocean steamer steadily coming on as she held her
way, seemingly in contempt of the warring elements, straight
down the centre of the river on her way to sea. It was the great
Morgan Liner, El Cid, which put to sea in the teeth of the tempest, her captain, with the grand confidence of the veteran
sailor in his trusty ship, preferring to risk the open water rather
than trust his vessel and cargo to the mercy of the angry waters
which were lashing the shore.

All along the Mississippi, on both banks, from Pointe-a-la-Hache to the Jetties, nearly a hundred miles, were strewn the wrecks of boats and luggers, the debris of houses, the bodies of animals, and the ghastly corpses of men and women and little children; while over it all nature, as if in shame of her own deeds, had spread a thick mantle of sea weed swept in from the Gulf of Mexico and a pall of the long marsh grass torn from the prairie which she had scourged in her fury.

On either side of the Mississippi river, in the marsh land between the river and the gulf, is a stretch of country threaded by numerous bayous, some known by names familiar to all, some with only a local nomenclature, and others so small that they are not deemed worthy of the dignity of a distinct appellation. Along these bayous, great and small, were settlements, places which the hardy fishermen called "home," where the smile of the wife and the prattle of the babes greeted their home-coming after the day of toil and often of danger. That section to the east of the river is known as "the Louisiana Marsh," while that to the west, comprising Bayou Cook, Bayou Shute, Grand Bayou, Grand Lake, Bayou Chato and many others whose names would mean nothing to the reader, was known by the generic name of "the Bayou Cook Country."

Here, the storm worked awful havoc on both life and property. While the loss of life was not so severe as at Cheniere Caminada, nor as great in proportion as it was at Bayou Andre (where none escaped), yet a death roll of over a hundred and fifty sent mourning and desolation into every household, save where there were no living left to mourn the dead.

Sunday is religiously observed by the Bayou Cook people. The little landing in front of their houses was crowded with luggers, smacks, small boats, skiffs and other craft used by them in fishing. These little boats were moored along side of each other and they were so numerous that they occupied a space of nearly 100 feet in the water.

The residences of the Bayou Cook people were not by any means handsome structures. They were built more for solidity than beauty. They were all one-story houses, strongly put together, for it was nothing extraordinary for a gale to sweep over the settlement at any time, and a lightly constructed house would never be able to stand these winds. Therefore, the Bayou Cook people knew from experience just what was safe, and accordingly they built their houses to stand an ordinary hurricane. The storm of that Sunday night, however, was no ordinary one. It was the worst blow that ever swept over that portion of the country, and the little houses that lined the banks of the curving Bayou Cook were blown away like so much chaff.

Just at what hour the disaster occurred that swept the settlement out of existence will probably never be known. It must have been in the neighborhood of midnight. The simple fishermen, their wives and their children were not asleep when the cyclone struck them in its full force. Experience had taught them that it was safe on the outside than in the inside of a house while a gale was in progress. This storm was such an unusual one that everybody in the village huddled together in the downpour of rain, and sent up many a prayer to the Almighty. When the storm broke in all its fury, house after house went down. The bayou began to rise at an alarming rate, and soon was level with the banks. Off in the distance could be heard the roar of the rapidly encroaching waves from the Gulf. Pandemonium reigned among the fisherman. Husbands forgot wives and mothers forgot children. It was a trying moment for everyone, and each and every individual felt that their lives were about to be sacrificed. Already many had been caught up by the wind and blown with terrific force against the wrecks of their homes, where they lay stunned and bleeding.

As the water in the bayou began to run out of its banks, the luggers, fishing smacks and other craft, which had been torn loose from their moorings, were swept ashore and mowed down the people by the dozens. Many of them were killed in this manner. The water rose with alarming rapidity. It soon covered the land, and gradually rose until it was waist deep. Those who had survived thus far clung to the debris from their homes, which was floating around in a tangled mass. Some succeeded in climbing on doors and windows, while others were satisfied to catch hold of a single plank to keep them from sinking beneath the foam-crested waves. In this manner they were swept back into the swamps, many to perish from drowning, having become exhausted and slid from their impromptu rafts, and sank beneath the dark waters. Others were dashed to pieces against trees and shrubbery, but the majority were borne out of sight, and many that were fortunate enough to survive the wind and water died from exposure before they could be rescued from their deplorable situation.

Among the men who escaped from Grand Lake were Cusue Murno of the lugger Atlas, Martel Zebilitzh and Pierre Zeblitizh of the lugger Bon Pere. Their lugger had gone to the city and they had been left in charge of the fishing camp. The storm had come upon them and they climbed to the roof of their cabin to escape from the rising waters. There they heard the cries of their terrified, drowning comrades, as the wrecked luggers went drifting swiftly past them in the storm and darkness, with their crews shrinking in mortal terror. Then their cabin was dashed to pieces and they were struggling in the water amid the storm and darkness. They kept together as they floated on the waves until one of them was dashed against an old pile or picket that was firmly fixed in the ground. He clung to it for his life and called his comrades. They all held to the picket until Monday evening, when the subsidence of the storm enabled them to swim to shoal water. They then wandered about in the marshes until Tuesday morning, and, finally reaching the railroad, boarded the train, barefooted, bareheaded and in a half-famished condition.

Mr. Fred Ziblich, a resident of Bayou Cock, sums up the storm, in a letter written to his brother, in New Orleans, two days afterwards, thus:

"The loss of life here is terrible, and it seems that there is hardly anyone in the neighborhood of Bayou Cook left to tell the tale of the storm and its destructive work. Only twenty people altogether have escaped from the storm in the bayou with their lives and they all tell a tale of horror and death. There is not a family but what has lost a member, or several members. Some families have been lost altogether, my wife is among the dead, but I don't know where they are and what has become of them. I was away from the house and could not get back in time to save them, if saving would have been possible. It is terrible, and words will never describe the horror, the destruction, the death and the great loss of property. There is hardly a house left in the whole neighborhood, and a great many of them have been carried away and lost altogether. Boats are washed upon the New Orleans and Fort Jackson Railroad and lodged there."

Three days after the storm Mr. Tony Anasawovich, another of the survivors, said to a reporter of the New Orleans Picayune:

"The story of the storm at bayou Cook and Grand bayou will never be truthfully told. It is impossible to paint a picture of the scenes of desolation. The entire country has been laid waste by the elements and there is scarcely a house left standing where there once existed happy homes and a prosperous colony. The camps have all been swept out of existence and the country is covered with every describable manner of debris and with the bodies of the dead, not all of which have yet been gathered for interment. It will probably be difficult to recover the bodies of all who were lost. Many of them were swept into the marshes. Families have been torn apart and many wiped entirely out of existence. It is difficult, however, to attempt to furnish names. Some of the missing may be still alive, and the confusion and terror are so great that people are as yet unable to account for their relatives and friends in view of the frightful experiences they have passed through."

The story of each and every bayou in the Bayou Cook country would be but a mournful repetition of the foregoing, changing the names of the sufferers. Everywhere were parents wailing for their children, and little ones crying the names of parents whose white faced corpses gazed with unseeing eyes to heaven from the matted marsh grass of the trembling prairie.

In the Louisiana marsh to the east of the Mississippi, the same destruction was wrought. There are but few bayous in this section, their places being taken by the chain of lakes which commences with Lake Pontchartrain in the rear of New Orleans, and continue until they reach the gulf, the principal one of which is Lake Borgne. From New Orleans south there runs into this country, on the left descending bank of the river, the Shell Beach railroad, which has its southern terminus at the little settlement from which it takes its name. Like its companion road on the west bank, the Shell Beach road suffered severely from the storm. Its track was washed and torn, and where it remained intact it was covered with debris and seaweed and the bodies of animals. It, too, had its quota of boats and schooners and luggers caught up out of the lakes and cast all along its line.

Shell Beach was more of a fishing camp than a settlement, and fortunately but few lived there. Some of the anglers of New Orleans had erected there a handsome club house at a cost of something like $7000. This building was in charge of Mr. Hebler who resided in it with his family. Here most of the people gathered when the storm broke, as it was the most substantial structure in the place. Mr. Hebler gave the following account of the storm there:

He said he had been there since 1884 and had seen no storm which was worth considering in comparison with the one of Sunday night.

At 5 o'clock Sunday evening the wind began to blow hard and probably reached the velocity of 40 miles an hour. The water rose about 12 inches and he took measures to secure the boats. At 10 o'clock the wind shifted to the northwest and the water came up to the floor. The sailboats went and the gallery was pulled down. At 2 a. m. the wind shifted to the northwest and there was 6 feet of water in the hall. The sewing machine, lamp and everything washed away and the doors went down and the floors were washed out in all the rooms but the kitchen. Soon only the uprights were left. The cistern was washed three miles from the house.

Two fishermen were in a willow tree from Sunday at 5 o'clock p. m. until between 2 and 3 Monday.

One Manilla man floated two or three miles and two others floated away in a pirogue and have not been heard from since. All the huts went, and there was only water and sky and rain during the early hours of Monday morning. Shell Beach is a desolate place.

Capt. Tony Juan, one of the residents of Shell Beach, who was absent at the time of the storm, gave to a reporter of the New Orleans Picayune a graphic description of the scene which greeted him on his return home the next day:

"When I reached Shell Beach," said Capt. Tony, "a scene of desolation greeted my eye. The magnificent clubhouse that formerly stood on the beach was a mass of broken and twisted timbers. Looking down the beach not one of the twenty camps that were formerly there could be seen. There was nothing to show that any buildings had ever stood there. My own camp, which was built near the clubhouse, and which I left in good order on Saturday, had disappeared.

Immediately upon my arrival I set about ascertaining whether any of the fishermen had been drowned. After a diligent search I managed to round up all those that were on the beach, and after noses had been counted it was discovered that seventeen persons were missing. Among this number was Martin Bonificiao and his family. The other twelve were men, and the belief is that they had all been swept back into the swamp, and it will require a thorough search to find their bodies. There is not the slightest doubt but that they are all dead, for if any of them had been alive they could have easily made their way back to the beach, as immediately after the storm had subsided the ten feet of water that covered the land flowed rapidly back into the lake. The survivors are so wrought up over the terrible ordeal they passed through that they had not the heart to institute a search for the missing.

I took down with me a lot of provisions, and I found that it was a Godsend to these people. They had not had one mouthful to eat since Sunday evening,and were in actual want, as there was not one bite to eat anywhere, the storm having swept away all eatables with their houses. They did not even have a fishing line; which would have enabled them to catch enough fish to appease their appetites. These people are now quarted at the house of C. H. Cyaley, which is six miles distant from the railroad terminus. The majority of them are nearly naked, their clothes having been blown away.

At Terre Aux Bœuf, Pescadorosville, Reggio, in short at every settlement or fishing camp or station, this sad scene was repeated.

At Pescadorosville, or the Island, as it is sometimes called, but two houses were left standing out of thirty.

At every point the personal effects of the people were washed or blown away, their houses were blown down, their fishing boats were staved and sunk, or carried so far inland by the immense volume of water which poured over the country, ⁿt they could not be returned to the water, and he who es-
ᵀ with his life, even though with broken bones, esteemed
ᵗʰᵉ ᵎᵛorite of fortune. In this country, too, each tuft
ᵗetation, half grass, half flag, might hide a man-
ᵇody, and at the bottom of every stagnant
ᵎing waters in the scored marshes, perhaps

HALF OF WHAT WAS LEFT ON CHENIERE.

might rest a ghastly corpse whose soul had winged its flight to the great beyond amid the howling tempest of that awful night.

For days after the storm the relief parties continually found the bodies of the dead, some of them the inhabitants of the region, others sailors whose vessels had been driven in from Mississippi Sound and the Gulf of Mexico and wrecked on the eastern shore of the "Marsh." Some were recognized and their last resting places were reverently marked; but many, very many, went to swell the list of the unknown and unclaimed dead.

CHAPTER IV.

'TWIXT RIVER AND LAKE.

While death was being dealt on the coast, the storm was not idle in the city of New Orleans. New Orleans is situated on the level land between the Mississippi river and Lake Pontchartrain; and, as the lake is joined to the gulf by waterways on the east, and the river in its sinuous winding as it nears the city approaches so close to the lake, it is almost an island. There are no bluffs or hills, not even the slightest elevation, to break the force of the wind, and so the storm had full play amid the houses of the Crescent City. But fortunately it was but the edge of the tempest that touched the town, and the blows that were struck there came from an arm already wearied by dealing death in the coasts below.

All day Sunday the rain had been coming down, with now and then a temporary cessation for a few moments; but the falling rain did not seem to lighten the burden of the clouds which hung low above the city as the day drew to a close, and as the darkness of night began to steal through the gray of the weeping day, the wind came moaning down across the waters of Pontchartrain, driving before it great windrows of inky clouds across a background of solid lead color, a phenomenon which boded no good for aught in the track of the storm of which it was the forerunner and prophet. As darkness fell upon the city and its myriad lights blazed out, here an electric spark that shone like a diamond on the bosom of the night, and, radiating in the distance, the gas jets scintillated like strings of jewels, the storm broke over the town. The water poured in an almost continuous sheet. In an instant, almost, it seemed, the streets were flooded; ditches and drains ran bank full, roadways were under water and sidewalks disappeared beneath the flood which stretched from house to house across the streets, broken only by the vehicles which cut through it hub deep, or the street cars which carried ahead of them a wave as boats at sea.

And above all roared the wind. Blast after blast tore through the streets, and the storm played the music of its weird fantasie on the Æolean harp of wires that swayed and swung and rang under the touch of the master musician, while at hundreds of points the blue-white sparks and jets threatened death to man who had dared to chain and harness the mysterious power of which they were the visible manifestation.

A serious accident occurred at the corner of Carrollton avenue and Second street. A telephone wire was blown down and lay across the trolley wire. The current from the trolley wire was transmitted to the telephone wire, and when a double team owned by Betz, the livery stable man, came galloping along, at 12.55 a. m., the horses ran against the fallen wire. Both horses were immediately killed and the driver had a narrow escape, being rendered insensible by the shock, from which it took him days to recover.

Trees were thrown down into the streets all over the city and travel was at first delayed and then interrupted altogether. The street cars ran at irregular intervals farther and farther apart, and then stopped. The charges of the cabmen rose higher and higher, until at last no offer of money could tempt them to brave the fury of the storm.

The telegraph wires were thrown down and for a time it seemed as if New Orleans would be cut off from the rest of the world; but two lines held out and served to carry to and from the city the pulse-beats of the busy world.

The beautiful grove of oaks at the United States barracks was almost destroyed, most of its largest trees being torn bodily from the ground, and the immense pole from which floated the garrison flag was snapped short off.

The church of the Messiah in the seventh district was demolished. The car sheds of the N. O. C. & L. road in the third district were blown down and the rolling stock extensively damaged.

The police telegraph was rendered useless and each precinct was a garrison cut off from all communication with supports.

At an early hour the swaying wires were crossed and a high tension current burnt out the switch board of the fire alarm service, leaving the city at the mercy of the fire bug.

At midnight one of the public markets for which New Orleans is famous, situated on Sorapuru and Tchoupitoulas streets went with a crash and was piled, a mass of tangled debris on its former site. An hour later the brick wall which had been its lower end followed the rest of the building; adding to the terror of the people in the vicinity. By this one incident the city lost $22,000.

By some inexplicable good fortune there was but one fatality in the city. Ulrich Boyer, a Boylan police officer, was the only victim of the storm. Boyer's beat was on the levee, in the vicinity of the Texas and Pacific Railroad depot. At the head of Henderson street, on the levee, the firm of A. K. Mitler & Co., were having erected a small structure to be used as an office. Between the hours of 11 and 12 o'clock Sunday night, when the wind was blowing at a terrible rate, the frame of the building was blown down and completely demolished. Boyer had been standing near the place, so as to secure shelter from the rain, which, at that time, was coming down in torrents. He was knocked to the ground by the falling timber, and there he remained for the remainder of the night beneath several heavy planks, suffering intensely.

At 7:30 o'clock Monday morning he was discovered and taken from his perilous position by Officer Roach. The officer was passing on the levee on his way to the Harbor Precinct Station, when a man's groans were heard by him. He traced the cries to the fallen building, and after a few minutes search he noticed Boyer. The man was barely able to speak. The only thing he said was to tell the time the accident happened and where he was injured. He complained of pains about the body and legs. Officer Roach telephoned for the ambulance. The man appeared to be slowly passing away, and as that vehicle was a little late in responding to the call, a wagon was secured, and in it the wounded man was laid and taken posthaste to the hospital. There it was found that his left thigh and arm were broken, and he was injured internally. His injuries were attended to, and he was placed in a ward. He died at 12:30 o'clock in the afternoon.

In Algiers, or the fifth district, that portion of the city on the west bank of the Mississippi, the damages were slighter.

The roof of the Woman's Benevolent Missionary Hall was blown off; also blowing down a colored church in Jefferson parish, with the fence and trees. This church was situated near Freetown.

The belfry was blown off the negro Methodist Church, and the slates off the Good Hope Baptist Church on Jackson street. The wind blew the church eight inches back from where it stood.

The walls of the old Planter's Oil Mills were blown down and damaged to a considerable extent.

The Women's Benevolent Missionary Hall is a two-story frame building, sitting back some distance in the yard. The wind played havoc with it, blowing the roof in as if it had been an eggshell. The house was a new building, and was still in process of construction.

On the river itself in front of the city the night was a wild one. The wind blew with terrific violence along the unprotected levee, and the men watching the interests of the shipping community were kept constantly on the qui vive to guard against loss of property.

About 9 o'clock the first accident occurred, when the big transfer steamer, Gouldsboro, of the Texas and Pacific road, started to cross the river in the teeth of the gale. The boat was loaded with passengers and freight cars for the Texas and Pacific road on the other side. The boat runs into a slip on this side, and no sooner had the vessel jutted her nose outside of the protection thus afforded than she was caught by the full force of the gale.

The current and the wind combined blew the boat down the river, and in less time than it takes to relate she was hurled against the fruit wharf of the Illinois Central road, at the foot of Thalia street. The mammoth engines of the big boat were incapable of stemming the fury of the wind and tide, and her starboard wheelhouse was ground into bits against the wharf. Her starboard bow was also battered in. The crew of the vessel managed to secure the boat before any further injury could be effected, and the passengers were safely housed.

The ferry boat, Edna, beat backward and forward in the river for two hours with the New Iberia excursionists on board, finally landing the passengers at a point above Louisiana avenue,

The ferryboat, Jerome Handley, plying between Race street and McDonoughville, broke loose from her moorings and was carried a short distance up the river, where she was blown ashore. The Handley while lying in this position parted her chains and settled into the river, where she now lies sunken. The Handley was owned by Capt. Thos. Pickles, was valued at about $10,000, and was not insured.

The steam launch Harry Shannon, valued at $1000, was lost while lying at the bank in Gretna. The boat lies sunk beneath the surface and cannot be raised.

The steamer Grace Pitt, owned by the New Orleans and Southern Railroad, lying just below the Good Intent Dry Dock, on the Algiers side, parted her lines during the gale and together with two barges, one lashed on each side of her, were blown up the river. Both of the barges were torn to pieces and the Pitt was carried ashore just below Morgan's depot at Gretna. The Pitt was valued at $6000, and was insured for $4000.

The big transfer W. S. Osborne, owned by the Illinois Central road, which was lying in retirement just above Louisiana avenue, was torn from her moorings during the storm of Sunday night and carried to the opposite side of the river. The Osborne sustained but slight damage to herself, but in tearing away from her fastenings did considerable damage to the steamer Ouachita, which was lying in retirement just above her.

There was trouble at the coal fleet moored at Willow Grove. The barges were moored close together, and the continual jostling caused the seams to start in all except the newest of the fleet. The laborers employed on the boats were kept busy pumping, but the water gained headway rapidly, and a barge belonging to T. J. Wood went down.

Joseph Walton's coal barge was the next to be lost; then the Munhall Bros. lost two coal laden barges. The total loss will amount to $11,000 or $12,000.

On the shores of Lake Ponchartrain in the limits of New Orleans are several pleasure resorts to which her people repair in the summer for rest and relaxation, and the cool breezes which blow in from the water. The principal ones are Milneburg, Little Woods, Spanish Fort and West End; the last being the largest and the most generally patronized. Here the people find music and bathing, fishing and boating; while numerous restaurants provide for the inner man.

The storm at these places was grand. At Little Woods the waves rolled clear across the little lakeside resort. The constant wash of the waves loosened the soil around the roots of the giant water oaks, and one after another they bent and fell from the force of the hurricane.

The houses were principally light structures and many of them were torn to pieces.

West End was a heavy sufferer. Trees were uprooted, platforms destroyed, small boats sunk, bath houses damaged, portions of the wharf torn up and plants and shrubbery whipped to ribbons.

The Southern Yacht Club was a considerable loser by the storm. About 300 feet of its walk from the end of the covered walk out to the club entrance was washed away. Otherwise, the club suffered little, if any. The rowing clubs on the east side of the basin all suffered. The landings of the St. John and West End clubs were washed away and the lumber piled about promiscuously or else lost altogether. The walk along the basin bank from one club to another is gone, and all that saved the West End club from sustaining the same losses as the others is the fact of the contractors for the revetment work having already removed the landing to make a place for depositing dredgings.

It was about 2 o'clock Sunday afternoon when the damage began to be done. The summer house nearest the east end of the levee blew away entirely and without warning. The summer house at the big bronze statue acted very singularly. The floor and posts were blown away so completely that no one has so far found even the splinters, and yet the roof fell where the floor had been, and seemed to be in almost as good condition as when new.

The many handsome yachts in "the pen" were jammed against one another and were rubbed and bruised, and the yacht Nepenthe, belonging to Mr. Richardson, the commodore of the squadron, was torn from her moorings and blown a mile up the canal.

Spanish Fort suffered less than any of the other places, but overthrown trees, wrecked stands, torn shrubbery and washed walks and roads showed that it had not escaped scatheless.

At Milneburg the dwellings were damaged to a considerable extent, one of them being completely demolished, as well as a bathhouse.

A number of skiffs were wrenched from their moorings, and were either foundered or dashed into bits against the numerous sunken pilings with which the Lake at that point abounds.

It would be tiresome and uninteresting to detail the number of craft thus destroyed.

The scene during the storm is thus described by an eye-witness: "In the distance the lake, churned into a thick foam by the fury of the wind, rose and fell in mighty waves, whose crests were cut off as with keen knives before they had attained their fullest height. The waves dashed against the revetment and railroad trestle with tremendous violence, and the spray flew full fifteen feet high in many parts of the long walk. The billows rolled toward the shore, sweeping almost everything with them, and hurling drift and wreckage inland. The shore was lined with the rough fringe of pieces of battered boats, houses and pilings, which ever and anon would be lifted a trifle further inland by a wave more powerful than its predecessors."

One of the most thrilling experiences of the storm, but one fortunately unattended by any casualty, was that of the New Camelia, the little steamer which plies on Lake Pontchartrain between Milneburg and Mandeville. The last named place is a little town in the pine woods on the north side of the lake where many citizens of New Orleans have their summer homes, the New Camelia being the means of communication. This little vessel is built like an ocean steamer, not like the ordinary steamboat of the southern waters; and to this, together with the coolness of her captain, William Hanover, is due the fact that another horror was not added to the already too long list of that fatal Sunday. Her story can be told no better than in the words of her captain. He said:

"When we left New Orleans Sunday morning we had about fifty passengers. The trip was made to the north shore without the occurrence of anything of interest. The passengers had a delightful time at the resorts, and we started on the homeward voyage shortly after 4 o'clock in the afternoon. At Mandeville it was blowing stiff then, but not much to speak of. No rain was falling. We had been out but a short time when the wind started to blow in earnest. The passengers began to feel the effects of the blow, and the ladies retired to the cabin, where everything was made as comfortable as possible for them. Rain fell in torrents after we had been out an hour, and the wind had increased to a gale from the eastward. The New Camelia behaved wonderfully well in the gale, and though the vessel rolled like a drunken man and pitched like a bucking broncho, no damage was done either to the vesssl or her machinery.

"About 6 o'clock we were in a position to land at Milneburg. The wind was blowing great guns and the water was running very high. The rain was so terrific that we could not see the wharf, and though I was anxious to land my passengers, I did not want to risk an accident that might prove fatal to all on board. The gale from the eastward made it impossible for a landing to be made without carrying away the wharf or tearing the boat to pieces, and finding things in that condition I determined to steam out into the lake. I told those of the passengers who asked me that I would again try by the light of the moon. We dropped anchor near the Spanish Fort and rode the gale until after 10 o'clock, when the moon began to shine. But its light was too feeble for me to try the landing in the teeth of the gale, and I gave over the attempt.

"The gale was a fierce one by this time, and the steamer began dragging her anchor. I ordered that steam be kept up all night, and kept the engines going, so as to take the strain from the cable. We dragged a considerable distance all the same, and toward morning steamed out about four miles from the Milneburg wharf to the westward. We rode the gale all night in safety and tried to land about 11 o'clock Monday forenoon, but owing to the presence of the wreckage to the east, could not make the wharf on that side. The wind was then from the northwest and too strong for us to land to windward.

"The passengers had been uneasy all night, and I thought best to take them back to Mandeville. This I did, and we arrived there Monday afternoon."

The next day the steamer safely made her wharf at Milneburg, landing her passengers and easing many a heart on shore that had ached with fear for loved ones tossed on the choppy seas of the shallow lake.

CHAPTER V.

ALONG THE GULF.

Along the northern shore of the Gulf of Mexico from New Orleans to Mobile runs the line of the Louisville and Nashville railroad, skirting the very edge of the waters, where the salt spray from the crest of the incoming rollers is dashed over the rails by every gale, running over the marsh on a bed built at an enormous cost and maintained by untiring labor, crossing the numerous outlets from the lakes to the gulf by bridges of steel and iron. Scattered along the line from one end to the other

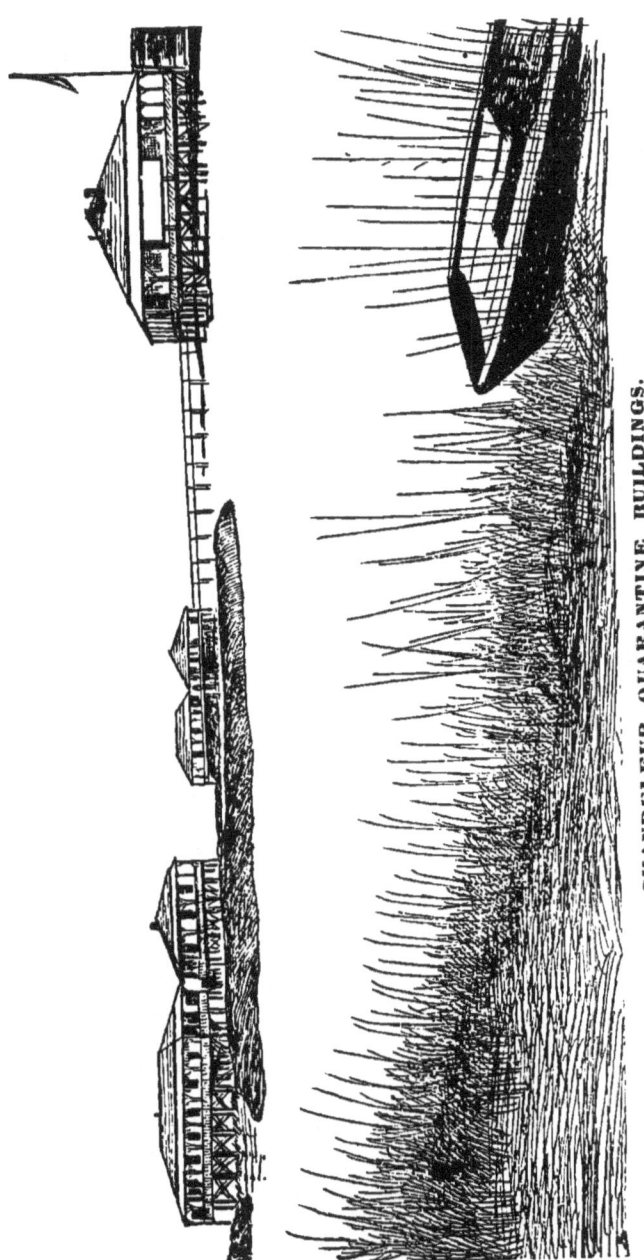

CHANDELEUR QUARANTINE BUILDINGS.

are little towns and hamlets, Lookout, Waveland, Bay St. Louis, Pass Christian, Biloxi, Scranton, Mississippi City, Ocean Springs and many others, forming almost a continuous stretch of houses fronting the beach, all popular summer resorts with the people of the South and known collectively in the parlance of New Orleans as "over the lake." Here in the hot summer months go the people of New Orleans to breathe the air redolent of the balsam of the pine, to lave in the waves that ripple on the shore and to revel in the cool salt breeze which sweeps in from the open gulf. This coast is protected in a measure by a chain of low-lying islands, mere banks of sand raised by the action of the waves; La Breton, Grand Grozier, the Chandeleurs, Cat Island, Ship Island, Horn Island and many others. All along this line, both on the islands and the mainland, the storm was felt in all its fury, and lives were lost by the score and thousands upon thousands of dollars worth of property was destroyed.

Probably the worst damage and loss of property was at Chandeleur island. Here was located the United States marine hospital quarantine buildings, in charge of Dr. G. M. Guitieras, with Dr. Chas. Pelaez, as assistant. At this point the fullest strength of the storm was developed, resulting not only in the almost complete destruction of all buildings on the island, but in a fearful loss of life. The velocity of the wind reached 100 miles an hour. The building and pier known as the disinfecting plant, supplied with all the modern appliances for the thorough disinfection of vessels from infected ports, was a complete loss, everything being washed away.

While the other buildings on the island were more or less damaged and uninhabitable, the largest house, connected with the main station was carried away, and the following persons drowned: Steward L. A. Duckert, of New Orleans; Nurse McKenzie, of Mobile; Seaman Muller, of Amsterdam, and two patients, one named Lazen, of the steamship Raversdale and Geo. B Salmis, boatman of the American bark Rebecca Goddard.

The buildings on the island were located so far apart that there was no communication, and it was impossible for the occupants to render asssistance to one another. The lighthouse was also wrecked to such an extent that the lighthouse keeper abandoned it. Miles of the island were completely washed away, and what little remains is liable to be completely submerged with little more than an ordinary high tide.

The damage by wind to the quarantine service alone at Chandeleur island will amount to nearly $100,000.

The disinfecting plant, which had been erected during the past year, together with the wharf and disinfecting apparatus, cost $17,000. The other buildings and improvements between $50,000 and $60,000, to which may be added about $30,000 for the steam transfer boat Wm. H. Welsh, Captain Jas. Delmas, which went aground at the north point of the island in 3 feet of water at high tide, with a draft of 7 feet. About forty head of cattle were also lost on the island.

Tuesday a Manilla sailor made his way to the Chandeleur Station from the fishing sloop Laura B., of New Orleans, which was wrecked in Grand pass. Out of a crew of seven men he was the only survivor, and when found on the island was in an unconscious and perfectly nude condition having been in the water over ten hours. The oyster lugger Rosalie, of Biloxi, is also known to have gone to the bottom with a crew of four men.

The American bark Rebecca Goddard, from St. Johns, lying at Quarantine, dragged her anchors about five miles from the station, and only saved the vessel from going ashore by cutting away the masts and all the rigging, sustaining a loss of about $5000 or $6000. The Henry T. Gregg had a similar experience and was completely dismasted, the loss footing up fully $6000. The Austrian bark Nikita, which was in quarantine at Chandeleur, was lost with all on board. She had a crew of about twelve men. The Norwegian bark Rogna was also dismasted.

Tuesday night the Henry T. Gregg took two Italian fishermen from a raft as they were drifting out to sea. Another raft also passed the vessel with three men on board, but the Gregg's small boats were so badly wrecked that they could lend no assistance to the unfortunates, and nothing has been heard from them since.

John Graham, who had charge of Dantzler's lumber barge Remus, said that the barge went to pieces and he was picked up by the master of the Simon. Before going to pieces the the schooner New Union passed within 300 feet of him with five men clinging to the bottom. It was blowing too hard to save them. A man named Hough, who was with Graham, was drowned. Andrew Olesen, who was on the bark Annie B., said that she struck early in the morning on Cat Island. Himself and four others went over on the lumber and drifted to the island. Before he got there one of the men was washed overboard. The captain and the rest of the crew are missing. A sailor told him he saw the captain go overboard. When they reached the island the sand blown by the wind drove them back to the water where they both clung to the trees. They were taken off next day.

Captain Roberts of the tugboat Julius Albert reported the day after the storm over a hundred dead bodies floating in the gulf between the islands and the coast. Among the lost was Louis A. Duckert, hospital steward, at Chandeleur. He was swept off into the gulf by the tidal wave amid the howling of the tempest. More than a week afterwards his body was found on a small island more than ten miles away. For days and days searching parties found bodies in the long grass of the marshes, and they were buried where they were found, swelling the list of the unknown dead. Miles off shore the odor of the decaying bodies told all too plainly that all of the dead had not been found.

At every little town along the coast there was tremendous damage to property and at many there was loss of life.

Jack Shepard, the assistant bridge tender on the Biloxi Railroad bridge, was washed overboard and drowned. His body was recovered the next day and buried at Ocean Springs.

The financial loss along the entire coast will foot up not less than $1,000,000.

LOUIS A. DUCKERT.

The canning interests suffered severely from the storm. Their losses in the aggregate amount to over $25,000. The Barataria Canning Company lost their wharves, engine-room, large lot of canned goods damaged, machinery, cans and other material. They estimate their loss at from $8000 to $10,000. Lopez, Dunbar's Sons & Co., oyster packers, lost about $10,000 on their factory plant and water craft. Wm. Gorenfle & Co., oyster packers, on the Back bay, estimate their loss at about $3000 and the E. C. Joulian Packing Company lost about $4000. The Biloxi Canning Company also located in the Back bay, lost from $3500 to $4000 in storm-swept buildings, damaged machinery and canned goods.

At Scranton, Miss., the waters of the river and sound rose rapidly, submerging the track of the Louisville and Nashville Railroad, carrying the schooners Franklin and Amelia upon the embankment of the railroad, where they were left by the water. The brig Mary C. Minor was carried into Lowery Island, about half a mile north of the railroad, and the brig Emma and schooner Taylor were stranded at Freutz shipyard. The charcoal schooner Webb capsized 200 yards south of the railroad.

The Lutheran and Methodist churches and four negro churches at Scranton were wrecked besides Odd Fellows' Hall was so badly injured that it is no longer safe. The large machine shop of T. C. Gatti was blown down. Mead Bros.' mill was unroofed and incalculable damage done to others.

In East Pascagoula the damage was much greater, as the whole road front was destroyed, the Catholic church being removed from its pillars and the Union Church completely destroyed.

At Lookout, the great fishing resort of New Orleans, the storm was awful. Boat houses were destroyed, boats were wrecked and the whole country inundated. Fortunately the main buildings, though rough, were strong, and the large number of amateur fishermen there escaped with a bad fright.

The following graphic description of the storm at Waveland, Miss., one of the prettiest watering places on the line of the L. & N. road, is from the pen of Mr. Henry P. Dart, a leading New Orleans lawyer:

"A moderate wind blew all Sunday forenoon, which roughened the sea somewhat, but the sky was clear and there was nothing to indicate unusual weather. About 1 o'clock, the wind changed to southeast, and with it came rain, increasing as the afternoon waned until at 6 o'clock it was quite dark and a stiff gale blowing.

The direction of the storm sent everybody indoors, and closed all openings toward the front. We are accustomed to rough weather at this season, and if any attention was diverted to it, it was not serious. Toward midnight, however, sleep was out of the question. The trees creaked and cracked. There was a deep booming along the shore, and over all the wind rushed and whistled and the rain pelted in torrents. Chimneys and openings of every kind leaked, and the town awaked and prepared for something to happen.

About 4 o'clock the first touch of light crept up, and then we saw that the sea had left its normal bed and was dashing over bluffs and pouring across roads, while beyond and ahead of all flew the scud as high as our trees. Just as day broke the sight was most impressive; the great waves swept unimpeded over the shore and broke in the road, with a mighty roar that could be heard above every other sound; the horizon seemed only across the way,—a mighty upheaval of water clouded by mist and full of spoil.

Between 2:30 and 5 o'clock the wharves and bathhouses succumbed, and soon there was not a stick of timber between sea and shore. The gale was then at its height and half an hour more it would have destroyed many a home. Just as it seemed that the sea would sweep houses and people away the wind changed round and blew equally against it. I saw the great rolling crests scatter their furious spray, then flatten out and suddenly recede; moment by moment the victory was made surer, and in two hours the watery giant was conquered, and we had nothing more to fear, as he lipped the shore far below his previous usurpation."

At Bay St. Louis, Miss., the storm began on Sunday morning about 8 o'clock with a heavy rain. The rain continued all day, and the wind increased in fury every hour. It rained and blew big guns all night, but the full force of the storm was not felt until about 5:30 on Monday morning. Then it blew a regular cyclone, and every bathhouse on the beach from one end to the other was swept away and hurled out into the raging waters. Trees along the beach were uprooted, while the roofs of nearly all of the outhouses were blown away. A negro church was unroofed and the roof thrown alongside of the building. Every yacht, schooner and small craft that was moored to the various landings were torn from their posts, and were either dashed to pieces against the ruins of the wharves or were blown high and dry ashore. Eight or nine large schooners were washed ashore, and either ruined or badly damaged; $250,000 would not cover the damage done the beach and Bay. So far as has been ascertained, but one life was lost, although many had narrow escapes from death.

Charlie Charlot, one of the crew of the schooner Centennial, which was wrecked in front of Mr. F. Butler's home, in Waveland, was washed away and drowned while clinging to the keel of the capsized vessel. The Centennial was under command of Capt. W. H. McDonald, brother of Hon. John McDonald, mayor of Pass Christian, and was anchored off the Pass. About midnight the anchor chain broke, and in making an effort to draw it aboard and get under way he was knocked overboard by the boom. From midnight until day he fought a terrible battle for his life. Many times he was on the point of giving up, and would have been drowned had he not secured a piece of timber on which to rest his body. About day he was washed on the drift of the broken railroad bridge and managed to crawl from that upon the bridge, that was still standing, but over which the waves were furiously dashing.

Manuel Marti and Johnnie Dougherty, draw bridge tenders, were not rescued until late Monday afternoon. When they saw the bridge was doomed, they opened wide the draw and thus saved themselves, while the bridge was washed away for many hundred feet on each side.

At Pass Christian the havoc was terrible. Every vessel in the vicinity except a small cat boat was wrecked; every wharf and bathhouse was washed away; houses were torn to pieces, and the waves rolled through it threatening to wipe it out of existence The damage here was over $100,000.

At Mississippi City, De Buys and Beauvoir (the home of Jefferson Davis), in fact all along the coast, the same story of death and damage was repeated. Houses destroyed, roads ruined, fences and outbuildings prostrated, the beach torn and seamed and scarred by the mighty pounding of the waves which rolled furiously in, bearing on their crests the timbers of wrecked vessels and the bodies of their drowned crews. Column after column of the newspapers was filled with lists of the vessels lost, and the dead were so numerous that only the number, not the names, were given in the reports. At the Rigolets, (the pass from Lake Pontchartrain to Lake Borgne) sixteen lives were lost,—three captains of vessels with thirteen of their crews. The schooner Angeline with her captain and crew disappeared; not a timber of the boat nor a single body of all who manned her were ever found.

The City of Mobile, the point where the Louisville and Nashville road leaves the gulf and strikes north, was a heavy sufferer. The damage here was in the neighborhood of a quarter of a million dollars.

Mobile is situated at the head of Mobile bay, where the river of the same name enters it. Like New Orleans it has its suburbs and water side resorts, where many thousands of dollars were invested. But not only these places were stricken by the storm. The water invaded the business houses on the principal streets, and thousands of dollars' worth of goods were damaged. A number of vessels were driven ashore; one steamer, after her passengers and crew escaped, was lifted on the crest of a wave and carried in and deposited across the "shell road," Mobile's chief drive. Every wharf and bath house on the western shore, from the city to the mouth of Dog river was swept away. On this same shore a singular effect of the storm was seen. In the memory of the oldest inhabitant there was not a time when it was not covered with logs and debris of all sorts, thrown there by the waters on their way to the gulf. The storm swept it bare and for the first time in the history of Mobile the western shore showed a clean beach of pure white sand. The handsome courthouse was damaged to the extent of three or four thousand dollars. The mills in the vicinity suffered severely, both in damage to buildings and machinery and in loss of stock. One merchant alone lost $4000 worth of salt. By a singular freak the wind took a piece of marsh about 40 feet square and 2 feet thick and turned it completely upside down, leaving a pond for ducks and a hill at the other side. Mr. Frank Ruter found a grand piano floating in the bay and brought it ashore; no owner could be found for it.

All the suburbs of Mobile, and the little hamlets near it suffered severely. The residence of Henry Seaman was carried away by the flood, himself and family on top of it. As they drove before the storm a huge alligator climbed aboard, and refused to vacate, though repeatedly clubbed over the head by Seaman. The family were rescued from their perilous position.

In the marshes around Mobile were numerous market gardens, most of them cultivated by Germans, who, with their families, lived in their little plots. They were devastated. Not only the crops, but the gardens themselves were utterly destroyed and the land reduced to the original marsh from which it was redeemed by the labor of these men. Nor was this the worst. For days after the storm abated the bodies of these poor people were found, where they had been carried by the waves or blown by the wind, in the stagnant pools which studded the marshes.

The heaviest sufferer from the storm was the Louisville & Nashville railroad. There was hardly a foot of its road from New Orleans to Mobile that was not damaged; and when it is stated that a large part of it is composed of long and costly drawbridges spanning "passes" which are really arms of the gulf, and that these were wrecked, it can be seen that damage meant destruction.

Of the Bay St. Louis bridge there only remained a half mile on the Bay side and the iron draw near the Pass, or east end; of the balance there was not a trace, not a stringer or rail left on the posts.

The Ocean Springs bridge at Scranton was badly damaged; three miles of track between Scranton and West Pascagoula entirely gone and roadbed more or less damaged. The track material was found in the marsh, scattered far and wide from its original position. One span of the long iron bridge at West Pascagoula was down in the river a total wreck, and the remainder of the bridge was damaged. The bridge across Biloxi bay, except the draw and about seventy spans, was washed away. The assistant drawkeeper was drowned. The tender saved his life by climbing upon the draw, whence he was rescued by lifeboats upon the subsidence of the waters. The bridge at Bay St. Louis was all lost with the exception of the draw and 170 bents.

There was over 7500 feet of the Biloxi bridge destroyed, while over a mile of the Bay St. Louis bridge was washed into the gulf. Every stick of the Back Bay trestle and every grain of the fill at the same point completely disappeared.

Between Gulf View and Claiborne, about a mile of the track was washed away, and there were also washouts at Rigolets and Lake Catherine, and between Rigolets and Lookout.

For a distance of two miles and a half between Micheaud and the Chef the track was in a bad condition. The heavy wind storm had driven the water from the gulf until it overflowed the tracks, and when it receded it had carried the earth filling between the ties with it. At Chef Menteur a worse state of things greeted the officials. The Lake Catherine fill

THE BILOXI BRIDGE.

was found to have been washed away for a distance of about 350 feet. This fill is at the place where the line crosses Lake Catherine, just beyond the Chef station. Instead of bridging the water it was filled in and boxed on either side. This filling had been washed away, thereby causing the tracks to sink into the lake.

Just beyond the Rigolets bridge the greatest washout ever happening to a railroad in the South occurred. As far as the eye could reach, the straight road bed could be seen and not a vestige of a crosstie or rail was anywhere. The hard road bed was smooth on the surface and a horse could

have been trotted along where the trains had been running on
the iron bands without encountering a single obstacle, except
the occasional gap where the sand in the road was soft and the
water made a small opening. Along the side of the track for
many miles a bayou about 12 feet wide runs within 10 feet of
the track. All the rails and crossties had been washed into
this canal and were buried out of sight. Every few hundred
feet the track, had been broken and the ends of the rails
were twisted out of all shape and bent and almost tied in
knots. This washout extended without a break to Lookout, a
distance of three miles.

But it would take too much space to describe all the damage in detail. Enough has been said to give an idea of what
it was. The scene just described was repeated over and over
again, mile after mile, almost to Mobile.

The telegraph lines were down everywhere, poles snapped
off or washed out of the ground, wires broken and twisted into
a tangled web, and all communication cut off; and a train
loaded with passengers was caught between two of the
wrecked bridges, unable to get back or go forward, and lay
exposed to that dreadful storm all night.

By a stroke of good fortune Mr. Charles Marshall, superintendent of the wrecked division, happened to be in Mobile,
the east end of the division, while his chief clerk, Mr. A. J.
Jacobs, was in New Orleans. Both immediately began work
from their respective ends of the wrecked division and by
laboring night and day reopened traffic in two weeks; the
lowest estimate made of the time necessary to do so being one
month. How it was done is best told in the words of Mr.
Marshall in an interview in the New Orleans Picayune the
day the road re-opened for travel.

"I was in Mobile," he said, "having gone over there to see
if I could arrange for the capture of the men who wrecked our
train at Gulfport, and also to look after the strike which had
not as yet adjusted itself, when the first news of the great
storm reached me. Late Sunday night I received the information from Scranton and Biloxi, that there was a great gale
blowing there, and danger imminent to our road, as well as to
the property and lives of the people. I was at the telegraph
office anxious to get all the news about it, for I was apprehen-
sive that if the storm was very severe that our road would
suffer, as it has done in the past. But I was not permitted to
get another telegram, for the wires were all down. Then I
knew that the mischief was to pay, and made all arrangements
to get out early Monday morning, to investigate the matter.
Monday morning arrived, and with it as fierce a gale as I ever
saw. The storm in this city was at night, between 10 and 3
o'clock, so I learn, but in Mobile the greater wind blew be-

tween 3 o'clock and daylight. I had my train all ready to go to
Scranton, at daylight, but the wind was so wild and seemed to
be hungering so to blow something away, that for a while I
hesitated in starting out. As its fury, however, did not seem
to abate, I deemed it best to go ahead. I had no trouble in
getting within a few miles of Scranton, and there I learned of
the vast damage done to our road all along the line. I went
right to work, as a matter of course, and there was work to be
done, as I found out later.

"As soon as I could, all arrangements were made for men
and material. Telegraphic communication was had with our
officials at the other end of the line, and, the situation realized,
material began to arrive. Much of it was in readiness to be
used, and much of it was not. I had no trouble in getting
men, but the proper kind of material was at first hard to secure. At last, however, after a few days, I had barges of it on
the bay, and a tug on hand to haul it about. The first thing
was to get matters systematized. I made Scranton a sort of
base of operations, and from there progressed along the line
as fast as the repairs would permit. Having gotten all the
needed material on hand, the work of repairs was conducted
smoothly enough.

"At Biloxi there was a crew of nearly 300 men, under the
supervision of the company's chief engineer, Mr. R. Montfort.
At Bay St. Louis, our superintendent of bridges, Mr. H. Bolla,
had charge of the work, and at Ocean Springs, Mr. Fay. At
each of the other points, there was an engineer of the road
stationed, and a gang of men placed at his disposal. In each
of these gangs there was the greatest system that could be es-
tablished. There were men to do every part of the work, and
these men did nothing else, except that which was assigned to
them. Sub-bosses were in charge of smaller gangs, all under
the direction of a head engineer.

"There was a pile driver at every bridge, and a crew of men
to work it. The pile-driving gang drove piles where needed,
and straightened up those which had been washed aside by the
storm. Most of the work consisted of the latter, the water.
though fierce enough, not being able to entirely drive the deep
driven piles from their position. Following on the heels of the
pile drivers came the stringermen, whose duty it was to place
the long stringers in position on the tops of the piles, upon which
the ties were to be laid. This done, along came the capping
men, those who fastened the stringers in position and made them
ready for the receipt of the ties. The next gang placed the ties
in position, another following fastened them as they should be,
while still another gang hauled the rails from the rafts and
barges underneath, and laid them in position. The next gang
nailed the rails in place and the following gang adjusted them to

the proper width. This placed the track in shape, and then along came the inspectors, who looked over the work and saw that it was all right.

"Thus was the work of repair carried on, a gang thus systematized being at each bridge of any importance, though most of them were concentrated at Biloxi, Bay St. Louis and Ocean Springs. At all the other less serious breaks smaller gangs, working under the same system, carried the repairs as rapidly as possible. You can readily see that with a force of 600 men, all thus systematized, when they all got down to business we made things move.

"Well, we had to," continued Mr. Marshall, "for time was worth to us the sum of $5 per minute—that is the company was being put to that much expense in the employment of laborers and in the loss from delaying of trains and the detention of business, or approximately that amount. As soon as one piece of work was finished another was begun. Having finished the work at Ocean Springs, which was nothing serious, without hardly even stopping for a meal the entire gang moved on as fast as possible to Bay St. Louis, where the same system was adopted and the work finished. We had some trouble on account of the barges containing some of the material being blown away, but they were soon recovered and gotten within easy access, having a tug at hand for all such emergencies. The work looked at first as almost a futile task for I never saw such wreck, ruin and devastation. Everything was torn all to pieces, the solidly built trestling and tracts in many places being blown from their positions intact and swept to the four winds of the earth. Some of our road, for all I know, is in the Gulf of Mexico 100 miles from land, much of it, perhaps, further away. I learn, however, that there is a string of the Bay St. Louis bridge 300 or 400 feet long off the coast some fifteen or twenty miles, on the Chandeleur island. Mr. Montfort is over there now, with a force of men, to see if he can't capture it and bring it back. All along the coast, on all the small islands, I understand there are strings of our track lying high and dry on the sands."

Speaking of the manner in which the night work was carried on, Mr. Marshall said.

"We had large iron baskets extemporized and hung from wires stretched along the line of operation. In these baskets was constantly kept burning a large bright fire of pine knots, for of this material there is an abundance there. The locomotives also, on both ends of the line, furnish us considerable light. It was rather a picturesque scene to see 400 or 500 men at work in the glimmering rays of a pine knot fire. The negroes, however, seemed to like the night work, and for several nights we accomplished as much good as during the day."

CHAPTER VI.

THE DEAD AND THE LIVING.

The whole gulf coast, from Barataria bay to Mobile, both banks of the Mississippi river, from Pointe-a-la-Hache to the Jetties, and the desolate marshes between were strewed with the bodies of the dead. Men, women and little children, drowned in the mad rush of the angry water, or mangled beyond recognition by the huge logs and house timbers which were borne upon the flood, or dashed to death against trees and piles and houses by the tidal wave, lay cold in death on the devastated fields, in the rank rushes of the marsh, in the depths of the moss-hung swamps and on the white sands of the seashore. Some lay dead by their own hearthstone, their life crushed out by their own rooftree; some were carried miles and miles from their homes; and some were swept out to sea, never to be found. Nor was it the dead alone who were thus carried away. When the sun rose on Monday morning it looked down on many a mangled and bruised form, in which there was yet just enough of life remaining to be conscious of its own suffering, and to realize the helplessness of its own condition and the narrow hope of rescue. Many of these were found in time to save their lives; but the burial parties found many another whose position told all too plainly that death had come only after many, many hours of suffering, in that awful solitude, with no witnesses save the foul carrion birds which circled aloft, waiting their hour, which they knew would come.

Many of these incidents will be told in their appropriate place in this work; now we are dealing with the number of the dead.

How many of these there were will never be known exactly, for all were never found. Some were swept to sea, some were carried into the trackless marsh or tangled swamp where the foot of man has never trod, and some found sepulture in the "trembling prairie" in graves dug by their own weight.

The following list gives the number of the dead found and buried at the places named; those marked as lost from vessels were seen by witnesses to go down to their death:

THE DEAD.

Cheniere Caminada...	822
Bayou Cook..........	24
Bayou Shute.............	75
Bayou Lafond...........................	100
Bird Island.............................	50
Bayou Andre (All Chinamen)..............	63

THE DEAD—continued.

Grand Bayou	16
Bayou Challon	40
Grand Lake	20
Cabanage	20
Near Shell Beach	17
Simon Island	15
Pearl River	10
Grand Isle	27
St. Malo (All Malays)	12
Bayou Dufon	11
Barthelemy	7
Grand Bank	4
Grand Prairie	4
Razor Island	5
Empire Mill	3
Oyster Bayou	3
Fort St. Philip	6
Point Pleasant	5
Hospital Bay	4
Faesterling's	3
Grand Bay	3
Old Quarantine	2
Bayou Chato	3
Nairn	1
Port Eads	1
Happy Jack	2
Nicholls Postoffice	4
Back Bay	1
Stockfelths	1
Sixty Mile Point	3
Devil's Flat	1
Bolivar Point	2
Socola's	7
Riceland	2
Chandeleur Island	100
Biloxi	1
Bay St. Louis	2
Mobile	12
Lost on Schooner Alice McGuigan	7
Lost on Schooner Angeline	6
Lost on Schooner New Union	6
Lost on Bark Rosella Smith	3
Lost on Lugger Young American	15
Lost on Bark Annie E. B	6
Lost on Sloop Laura B	6
Lost on Lugger Three Brothers	3
Lost on Sloop Alice	2
Lost on Barge Hero	1

THE DEAD—continued.

Lost on Barge Boss......................	1
Lost on Schooner Bertha..................	3
Lost on Lugger Sunny................	3
Lost on Schooner Premier.................	5
Lost on Schooner Centennial.	2
Lost on Schooner Pecourt..................	5
Lost on Unknown Schooner..............	3
Total........... 1607	

To show that the foregoing figures are not guess work, the following list of families at Cheniere Caminada is given, showing the number of saved and lost in each family, so far as the names could be ascertained:

	Saved.	Dead		Saved.	Dead
Rodolph Cheramie	10	..	Victor Busere.........	1	7
Louis Malcon...... ..	1	4	Jack Sponge..........	..	8
Pierre Colin	7	.	Joseph Sponge	1	5
Silis Viger	7	1	Ouace Dantin.........	1	6
Louis Chabert	10	..	George Dantin	..	6
Veronnique Pitre	1	2	John Michel..........	1	4
Prospere Terrebonne ..	4	5	Pierre Nicol......	..	9
Dupres Terrebonne....	2	..	Talesfort Bonnamour..	..	3
Louis Terrebonne	2	2	Antone Allanda.......	1	5
David Pitre	7	4	Pierre Amont	1	2
Mme. Richard Pitre...	4	..	Orelien Crosby........	..	8
Didier Pitre	2	..	Mr. Carmody	..	1
Augustin Gaspard ..	6	..	—. Tracy	..	1
Ernest Gaspard.......	3	5	—. Joseph............	..	1
Oleus Cheramie.......	8	..	—. Carpenter.........	..	1
Felicien Lefort	7	..	Oscar Terrebonne.... .	4	I
Harisonne Gaspard....	..	7	Dr. Frederick Collin	..	2
Elfege Lefort.........	5	..	Licar Jambon........	2	2
Alexis Lefort	9	..	Andre Pizani......... ..	..	5
Millen Lefort.........	2	..	Leopold Pizani	..	7
Esebe Crosbe.........	2	..	Maick Allen	..	5
Adrien Lefort	4	..	Michel Terrebonne....	7	1
Borgard Viger........	8	..	Michel Jambon	7	..
Armand Crosbe.......	5	1	Theodule Terrebonne..	1	4
Julien Crosbe.........	3	..	Leon Cherriot	1	5
Nicolas Turol	3	..	Picha Sponge.........	5	..
Tele Terrebonne	14	..	Lucien Terrebonne ...	8	..
John Rebstock........	11	..	Manuel Incalade......	2	..
Camil Rebstock.......	3	..	Philip Billili..........	1	6
Arthur Terrebonne....	2	..	Marius Perrin	1	4
Pierre Turol..........	4	..	Chapha Danlin........	..	2
Etienne Curol	2	..	Odras Sponge.........	3	..

	Saved.	Dead		Saved.	Dead
Andres Curol	9	3	Lucien Theniat	7	..
Melfort Gaspard	6	..	Leo Amandin	5	..
Melfort Arnodin	3	7	Belente Terrebonne	2	3
Livode Pitre	6	..	Rudolph Terrebonne	4	..
Auguste Macolm	6	..	Didemi Darbin	..	2
Mme. Malcom	2	..	Orelier Oroby	..	7
Mme. Justin Pitre	6	1	Mme. John Polket	5	..
David Pitre	2	..	Opil Bouziga	..	3
Leodgard Pitre	1	1	Clement Bouziga	5	..
Bebe Labave,	4	..	Romain Delgrandil	5	..
Augustine Pitre	2	5	Mme. Dom. Bouziga	2	4
Marc Pissiola	3	..	Miguel Lanane	3	2
Dupres Terrebonne	8	..	Alexis Terrebonne	..	3
Aisere Pitre	5	10	Leopold Guedry	..	5
Jerazime Dantiu	3	..	Thomas Valena	..	7
Thomas Alario	3	7	Charles Lafont	..	4
John Kilgin	1	6	Charles Lafont, Jr	1	4
John Sanamon	2	5	Pete Lafont	1	4
Mme. Jacko Terrebonne	4	..	Theogeni Lafont	1	2
Steph Pitre	2	..	Theophile Guedry	..	2
Raimond Terrebonne	1	6	Blanchard Guedry	2	..
Aloxanere Anselm	5	..	Lee Demer	6	..
Robert Martin	6	.	Manuel Terrebonne	5	6
Guillaume Martin	5	..	Joe Boudro	1	5
Jos Martin	11	..	Dr. Frey	..	4
Jerazime Dantin	9	..	Alexis Crosby	..	3
Octave Dantin	5	..	Pit Labove	5	..
Francois Sandras	3	..	Ovide Petit	..	7
Singesse Terrebonne	8	..	Michel Never	1	..
John Stout	2	..	Clebert Boudro	5	..
Paul Malgom	1	5	Mme. Faustin Boudro	3	..
Charles Gilbot	4	..	Dupret Lizard	4	..
Felicien Sandras	1	2	Ernest Angelleto	6	..
Alexis Sandras	4	..	Ozeme Cherami	8	..
Besinthe Sinblanc	7	..	Julien Boudro	6	..
Pierre Grimaud	2	..	Faustin Boudro	2	..
Mme. Victor Sandras	5	4	Clemene Claws	3	7
Thomas Martin	6	..	Enoch Claws	1	3
John Miller	3	..	Victor Arnodin	8	..
Frank Gilbert	5	4	Jos. Ortis	1	4
John Hadje	1	..	Alexis Serriot	..	5
Jeck Fallen	1	..	Armand Palket	1	4
Mme. Exavier Sandras	1	..	Antoine Volence	..	3
Claude Gilbos	1	6	Zephirin Duet	..	5
Jos. Lafont	1	3	Jos. Terrebonne	2	1
Andre Gilbot	..	2	Adam Sauveur	..	3
Mme. Joseph Cotton	4	..	Andre Collin	..	3
Jos. Gamesse	3	4	Mme. Ducos	..	3

	Saved.	Dead.		Saved.	Dead.
Gaspard Sicard..... .	1	3	Louis Broussard	1	5
Constatin Itros	1	6	Wilfred Pitre.........	2	3
Ernest Lafont........	5	..	Donnatien Coron	8	..
Eward Terrebonne....	3	1	Join Valence..........	1	6
Etienne Terrebonne ...	8	..	Louis Lafont........	1	9
Henry Gardey	8	..	Felix Pisanie	8	..
Dupre Terrebonne	..	10	Andre Pisanie	4	..
Louis Gurdey	..	6	Lesta Cheramie.......	..	6
Lorence Terrebonne...	..	7	Cirlaque Prospery.....	3	2
Bonnard Jambon	9	..	Leonce Prospery......	1	3
Raphael Pitre	4	..	Antoine Valence	..	10
Jos. Pitre	9	..	Mme. Jos. Incalade....	2	..
Adam Duet....	7	1	Theodore Crosbe.....	2	..
Adrien Pitre	6	..	Albertine Pisanie	2	7
Auguste Pitre	..	5	Theodore Pisanie	1	5
Dede Lafont..........	3	4	Martin Bonne	6	..
Brou Brankly	3	9	Joseph Lefort	..	3
Francois Bartelleme...	2	7	Jacques Collin........	5	..
Auguste Bonamour....	1	11	Alfred Collin	5	..
Batiste Abillet........	4	5	Mme. Peltier	2	..
William Reed........	1	8	Filazaque Collin	5	..
W. Corron...........	4	..	Ernest Lefort	8	..
Pierre Dantin	1	1	Adrien Sarol	3	..
Dorcily Dantin........	..	7	Noel Lefort..........	8	..
Etienne Perrin	3	3	Alice Lefort	6	..
Emile Angellet........	2	5	Julien Lefort	7	..
Etienne Perrin	1	3	Leonce Pitre	4	..
Alcide Pisanie	..	3	Felicien Collin	6	..
Hyppolyte Ellein......	2	4			

RESCUE AND RELIEF.

From the character, direction and intensity of the storm in New Orleans the residents of that city apprehended that great damage had been done in South Louisiana, but no one dreamed of its extent. And while it was believed that much property had been destroyed and that perhaps a life or two had been lost by the wrecking of vessels, there was not an idea of the utter destruction and terrible loss of life which had occurred, consequently there was no concerted action looking to relief until Wednesday afternoon. That afternoon the lugger Good Mother, of Cheniere Caminada, the only vessel of that place which was not wrecked, reached New Orleans with the news of the dreadful calamity. Captain Terrebonne, her commander (a hero who had saved some three score lives during the storm), appealed to the people to go to the rescue of the survivors. The response was instantaneous. The lugger landed in front of the French Market, and before her captain had concluded his story the merchants and residents of that vicinity began to gather food and clothing. They loaded the Good Mother with their contributions and she started on her return trip. This boat succored one hundred and forty families. Of course the news reached the newspaper offices immediately, and was promptly bulletined. But bulletin-

ROBERT BLEAKLEY, Chairman Relief Committee.

ing the news or sending boats after further information did not satisfy the New Orleans papers. The New Orleans Times-Democrat chartered a boat, loaded her with supplies and sent her down Bayou Barataria. The New Orleans Picayune immediately chartered the steamer Emma McSweeney, loaded her with a cargo of food, clothing, medicines and water, and sent aboard her a complete crew with a staff of helpers, doctors and reporters, with orders to first relieve the distress and then to get and bring in the news. Loaded to the guards the McSweeney swung out into the stream and departed on her errand of mercy.

That night several members of the Commercial Club (one of the leading social clubs in New Orleans) held a conference and the result was the following call, which appeared next morning in all the papers:

"The citizens of New Orleans are invited to meet in the rooms of the Commercial Club, 152 and 154 Canal street, at 12

THE GOOD MOTHER.

m. to-day to take immediate action toward aiding in the rescue of those who may be still alive but helpless at Cheniere and Grand Isle.

"ROBERT BLEAKLEY, President."

In response to this call a meeting was held at the appointed time and an executive relief committee with full powers was appointed, with Mr. Bleakley as chairman. This committee went immediately to work. Funds were collected, supplies purchased, medicines obtained and volunteers for relief parties enlisted. One party was sent by rail down the bank of the Mississippi to relieve the distress there; the steamboat Gamma was chartered and sent with clothing, food, medicine, water, surgeons and searching parties down to the Barataria section, and the steamer Alice, similarly equipped, was dispatched through lake Pontchartrain to the Louisiana Marsh and the gulf coast and its islands.

The Times-Democrat sent out the steamer Amelia Harvey on a similar errand down Bayou Barataria.

THE PICAYUNE'S RELIEF BOAT.

The French Market Protective Association organized a committee with Mr. John Alsina as chairman, and it dispatched similar aid by luggers. Boatload after boatload of necessaries was sent to the stricken section, and well it was that it was done, for everything was gone; in many instances the storm had torn even the clothes from the backs of the survivors, leaving them as naked as when they came into the world.

The various commercial organizations of New Orleans appointed committees to raise funds, in which they were eminently successful, and the contributions poured in. The Citizens' Relief Committee issued the following call, which was iberally responded to :

THE CITIZENS RELIEF COMMITTEE'S BOAT.

To the People of New Orleans : The committee for the relief of the storm sufferers request donations from the people of articles of wearing apparel for both adults and children, shoes, hats, blankets, etc., all of which are urgently needed. Send to 126 Camp street, opposite Lafayette square, or notify committee at that number, and articles will be sent for.

ROBERT BLEAKLEY,
Chairman Executive Committee.

JNO. C. WICKLIFFE, Secretary.

The New Orleans Board of Trade sent out the following appeal :

NEW ORLEANS, October 5, 1893.

The awful calamity which has overtaken the residents of the islands and coast near our city should appeal to the charity of all our citizens.

Food, medicine, and the means of assisting those unfortunates are 'necessary immediately, and the Board of Trade urges liberal contributions of cash and supplies, which will be distributed by the executive committee of the Board of Trade, of which Mr. Hugh McCloskey is chairman.

Each member of the following committees is authorized to solicit and collect subscriptions as stated above :

Provisions—Hugh McCloskey, Max Schwabacher, Simon Pfeifer.

Grain and Naval Stores—F. J. Odendahl, Jno. F. Simpson, Jno. T. Gibbons.

Rice—Jos. Buhler, F. G. Ernst, Jno. A. Hubbard.
Grocers—W. L. Saxon, I. H. Stauffer, Jr., Nicholas Burke.
Coffee—Chas. Dittman, E. P. Cottraux, A. L. Arnold.
Esculents—Henry Kahn, Leon Bloch, Martial Casse.
Brokers—W. H. Beanham, Wm. A. Gordon, D. R. Graham.

JOHN M. PARKER, President

HY. H. SMITH, Secretary.

And on the next day sent the following telegram:

To the Commercial Exchanges at Chicago, St. Louis, Cincinnati, Kansas City, New York, Philadelphia, Boston, Baltimore, Pittsburg, Minneapolis, St. Paul, Omaha and other places :

A terrible disaster has destroyed a majority of the inhabitants of the islands and marshes adjacent to this city, and the survivors are left penniless, their stock, houses, boats and means of livelihood gone, and they are in dire distress.

The people of Louisiana will bury the dead and feed the starving, but appeal to a generous public to assist in contributions which will enable thousands of deserving people to again follow their avocations and support their families.

Subscriptions of every character will be thankfully received and be disbursed by the executive committee of the Board of Trade, acting jointly with committees of the other commercial bodies.

John M. Parker. Jr.,
President Board of Trade.

The Red Cross Society of Louisiana, fully alive to the emergency, issued the following call :

Red Cross Society of Louisiana, }
New Orleans, Oct. 4, 1893. }

To the Public :

The Red Cross Society of Louisiana, of which Miss Clara Barton is the national executive, does hereby issue a call upon the public generally for subscriptions and contributions in aid of the sufferers from the recent storms in Southeast Louisiana, who are at present without food or shelter. The society requests that all subscriptions and contributions be made to John M. Coos, treasurer, at No. 2 Tchoupitoulas street.

J. B. Vinet, President,
E. K. Skinner, Secretary.

The various secret societies sent in their contributions; the Southern Pacific Railroad sent a check for a thousand dollars; the Grand Opera House, the Academy of Music and the St. Charles Theatre each tendered a benefit, the gross proceeds of which went to the fund; the pupils of the public schools gave their pocket money to the fund, thirty, forty and fifty dollars being sent in by each school; the city council of New Orleans voted $2500 to the fund and the individual members added a handsome donation from their own pockets. Replies to the appeal made by the Board of Trade began then to come in. It is impossible to particularize, for the contributions came from all over the country from individuals and organizations, especially the commercial ones, and were promptly applied. The churches of all sects and denominations set apart a special Sunday for collections and realized a large sum which was turned over to the committee.

The Stevedores and Longshoremen's Benevolent Association, an organization of laboring men, contributed one thousand dollars of their hard-earned wages.

Soon the various organizations recognized that relief could be more effectually given under one directing head and all of them were merged into the Citizens' Central Storm Relief Committee, of which Mr. Bleakley was chairman, which committee is still in existence and at work when this book goes to press. This committee worked in conjunction with the police juries of the parishes of Jefferson, Plaquemines and St. Bernard in which

THE RED CROSS HEADQUARTERS.

the devastation occurred. Not only were the immediate necessities of the people supplied but they were assisted to rebuild their homes and to raise, relaunch or repair their wrecked boats and were placed in a position to again become self-supporting.

But there were some instances of individual action which should be recorded.

Mrs. Ludwig, whose general store has long been known to nearly all the fishermen along the Gulf coast, dealt out goods to all who called for them, wholly regardless of their ability or inability to pay for them, until her store was completely emptied, the only person she refused being a man who desired to buy out her entire stock of certain necessities with a view of making a "corner" on them.

Mr. George Jurgens, a New Orleans merchant, who owned an orange farm on the lower Mississippi, went down on Monday morning to see to what extent he had been damaged. When he reached there the suffering and dead made him forget his own affairs. A few of his houses had withstood the storm. He filled them with sufferers, he divided among them every ounce of food on his place. He then hurried to New Orleans and sent down at his own cost, food, clothing, bedding and medicine. Then covered with mud, he appeared before the first meeting of citizens, told of the destitution, and then went immediately back at the head of a relief party.

The store of Mark Cuessiola at Grand Isle was wrecked but the spirit of the owner was not destroyed. He had suffered, but others, he knew, who could less afford to suffer, had suffered even more. Bright and early the next morning he made an inventory of his goods and found about $700 worth that were fit for use. He summoned his neighbors and gave them all that he did not himself actually need for a day or two.

Fred. Stockfleth, a store keeper of the lower Mississippi threw open his house and his store to the sufferers and gave away almost his entire stock. One of the sufferers among the scores relieved by Mr. Stockfleth voiced the sentiments of all when he said:

"I was stark naked, bleeding, and so hungry I could scarcely stand. He took me in and fed me and clothed me. What he did for me is but a repetition of what he did for every sufferer. Men like him are rare. He did more than any other three men in this section for the sufferers, and the saved remnant of the stricken people of Austria will ever be mindful of what he has done for us. God bless him."

The generous response to her appeal in her hour of need will ever be remembered in Louisiana. It knew neither sectional lines nor contiguity of situation, but came from the entire country. Americans were in distress and Americans came to their assistance.

CHAPTER VII.

LAST ISLAND.

Louisiana has had two horrors preceding this terrible calamity which resembled it but did not near approach it in loss of life.

On the night of October 4, 1886, a cyclone accompanied by a tidal wave swept down upon the settlements on Johnson's Bayou and Sabine Pass in Southwestern Louisiana, utterly ruining the country and killing about fifty people.

A thrill of horror went through the State, and relief was promptly given.

Her other disaster, known as the destruction of Last Island, more nearly approached the present one. Like it, it occurred on Sunday night, the date being August 10, 1856. Last Island lay west of Cheniere Caminada and Grand Isle, and, like the last, was a popular summer resort. When its storm occurred it was crowded with the representatives of the wealth and fashion of the Crescent City, and the loss of life was frightful. It was swept out of existence, the water rolling over it ten feet deep, and all that is now left of it is a narrow spit of sand. We reproduce the account of the disaster as it appeared in the New Orleans Picayune of August 16, 1856. This was the first account published of it, for news traveled slowly in those days.

"Statement of rescuing party returned from Grand Isle :

"They inform us that the storm commenced about 10 o'clock on Sunday morning, and a faithful picture of the calamity they declare to be beyond realization. The gale did not abate until Monday morning, and then the rain continued almost without intermission up to the time of their leaving the island, at times the wind rising pretty strongly again. The number of the victims they estimated at over 200, at least 182 having been already counted. The island was swept by 2 o'clock on Sunday, having been overflowed between noon and that hour. The wind blew first from the north and the northern part of the island was then overflowed. Next the wind came from the east, which beat the water off from the north side of the island; afterwards the wind shifted to the south, and then the island became overwhelmed by the water of the gulf. Horses, cattle and even fish lay strewn dead about the island among the victims of the storm. It is believed that many bodies have been washed out into the gulf.

"The following is a letter written by a survivor of the disaster:

"BAYOU BOEUF, Aug. 14, 1856.

"Dear Pic—You may have heard ere this reaches you of the dreadful catastrophe which happened on Last Island on Sunday, the 10th inst. As one of the sufferers, it becomes my duty to chronicle one of the most melancholy events which have ever occurred. On Saturday night, the 9th inst., a heavy northeast wind prevailed, which excited the fears of a storm in the minds of the many; the wind increased gradually until 10 o'clock on Sunday morning, when there existed no longer any doubt that we were threatened with imminent danger.

"From that time the wind blew a perfect hurricane; every building upon the island giving away, one after another, until nothing remained. At this moment every one sought the most elevated point on the island, exerting themselves at the same time to avoid the fragments of buildings which were scattered in every direction by the wind.

"Many persons were wounded, some mortally. The water about this time (about 2 o'clock p. m.) commenced rising rapidly from the bay side and there could no longer be any doubt that the island would be submerged. The scene at this moment forbids description, men women and children were seen running in every direction, in search of some means of salvation. The violence of the wind, together with the rain, which fell like hail, and the sand which blinded their eyes, prevented many from reaching the objects they aimed at. At about 4 o'clock the bay and gulf currents met, and the sea washed over the whole island. Those who were so fortunate as to find some object to cling to were seen floating in all directions. Many of them, however, were separated from the straw to which they clung for life, and launched into eternity; others were washed away by the rapid current and drowned before they could reach their point of destination.

"Many were drowned from being stunned by scattered fragments of the buildings, which had been blown asunder by the storm. Many others were crushed by floating timbers and logs, which were removed from the beach, and met them on their journey. To attempt a description of this sad event would be useless. No words could depict the awful scene which occurred on the night between the 11th and 12th insts. It was not until the next morning, the 12th, that we could ascertain the extent of the disaster.

"Upon my return after having drifted for about twenty hours, I found the steamer Star, which had arrived the day before, and was lying at anchor, a perfect wreck, nothing but her hull and boilers, and a portion of her machinery remaining. Upon this wreck the lives of a large number were saved. Towards her each one directed his path as he was recovering from the deep, and was welcomed with tears by his fellow-sufferers, who had been so fortunate as to escape.

"The scene was heart-rending; the good fortune of many a poor individual in being saved was blighted by the news of the loss of a father, brother, sister, wife or some near relative.

"I will not prolong the detail of this unparalled catastrophe, but will give you the list, as correctly as I could obtain it, of those who were lost."

CHAPTER VIII.

PATHETIC INCIDENTS.

The story of the storm would be incomplete without a record of some of the many acts of heroism which shine out from that background of horror, and a recital of some of the pathetic incidents which brought to the eyes of stalwart men tears of which they were not ashamed. All of them will never be known, for many a hero died with those he tried to save, and many an incident whose pathos would have moved a stoic left no witness alive to make it known. Nor is there space in a work of this description to record all that are known. But a few, culled here and there at random from different sections of the stricken country, are here related.

Trainmen and passengers on the New Orleans and Gulf railroad the day after the storm, saw a picture of a mother's courage and endurance they will never forget. The train was moving slowly through a stretch of country below the Crescent City where the wind had played sad havoc, and had made of that section of Louisiana, already a dreary, repulsive place, a scene that would be a fitting addition to Dante's Inferno. The stagnant waters of the marsh between the railroad and swamp beyond had risen almost to the tops of the low latania bushes and weeds, and on its foul surface the bodies of animals drowned by the tempest, were floating. Against the dark back ground of the forest with its uprooted and twisted trees, from which the gray moss fluttered in tresses yards long, the figure of a woman was outlined. A woman, a mother, with a child in each arm and a bundle in a sheet which she held in her teeth, in such a spot, sent a thrill of horror over all who saw her. In the swamp from which she came, few hunters would have dared to penetrate, for it was a veritable jungle in which many dangers lurked, and the green scummed water in which she was wading almost to her waist, shoving aside as she went, the matted weeds and bushes in whose shelter reptiles hid, seemed too foul and horrible for human being to enter and not be overcome by its noisome caress. But mother love had been stronger than that heroine's fear of the animals that shrank and snarled in the dense swamps, or the reptiles that she knew were all about her in the stagnant water through which she waded, and straight toward the railroad she made her way, and reached it with no injury save that of exhaustion. The train had been stopped, and willing hands pulled the brave mother aboard. She placed the children she held in either arm on the car floor, then tenderly laid the bundle in the sheet she had carried by its corners in her teeth, on a seat, and as a faint wail came from it, she carefully drew from its snowy wrapping a tiny babe that cooed and laughed when clasped to the mother's bosom, as if it were safe in the home nest that had been washed away by the flood. This heroine had travelled two miles through swamp and marsh land with her three children, and after passing through dangers that make brave men shrink to think of, guarded by the Almighty, she saved herself and her babes.

By the flickering light of an oil lamp in Stockfleth's store and in the "still watches" of the Sabbath morn, one week after the storm, Maximillian Duplease told the story of the wreck of his camp on Cheniere Ronquille. He said:

"My camp is twenty miles from here. On Sunday night the weather was bad, and I knew trouble was going to occur. At 8 o'clock it was bad, and between that hour and 10 I went through years of agony. All night long I fought for my life and for the lives of those dear to me. At 10 o'clock the camp went to smash and we all fell into the roaring waters. When I came to a bit I found that my wife had the two children, one gripped in her teeth by the clothes and the other thrown across her shoulder, The water was breast-high and the footing, you may imagine. very bad. My kitchen table came floating by and I seized it, and on it I placed my wife, my eldest child being in her arms, while I took the infant on my left arm. With my right arm I encircled a post, and the table was kept in position by my wife, who also gripped another upright timber. From 10 o'clock till daylight we stayed there, fighting for our lives, every now and then being overwhelmed with water, till we thought the end was near.

"On Monday morning the water subsided Then I went to hunt for a boat. There was not one to be found and until Thursday we were prisoners on the Cheniere, with nothing to eat or drink, save brackish salty water. On Thursday I found a skiff, and, after kissing my wife good-by, I started for Grand Isle, distant fifteen miles. I have a sister there and knew I could get help from her. At Fort Livingston I met Louis Valdon and Theo. 'Blackberry' in a skiff, and they, knowing me well, went to Cheniere Ronquille and carried my family to my relatives. Then I came on here to look after my other relatives. There were six of them; now there is one," and here the poor fellow broke down and wept freely.

Michael Trantovich, a Slavonian, had a frightful experience. His family consisted of his wife, Amelia; four sons, Michel, aged 21; Ura, 16; George, 8, and Nick, 5. His sailor, Andrew Kuzzi, aged 26 years, was also in camp with the family. About 11 o'clock Sunday night the house was demolished. Above the din he could hear the heart-rending cries of his wife. He caught a post and seeing his son George swept along within reach, he grasped him.

He then saw his son Ura, clasping the little fellow Nick, supported by another post. A heavy swell washed George from

WHERE BONZIGA SAVED THIRTY LIVES.

his embrace, while the continuous overwash of waves drowned the little fellow Nick in the arms of his 16-year old brother. Desperate over the loss of his cherished ones, the father called out to his sole surviving son: "Farewell, Ura, I go to join your mother and brothers." He loosened his grip on the log and sank beneath the waves. The current carried him immediately alongside of the post on which the boy Ura was hanging. Filial devotion lent strength to the boyish arm as he reached out, and catching his father by the hair, he elevated his head above the surface of the water. The boy's pleading and piteous cries moved the father, and with the reaction came a return of parental love for the living. He reached out and caught the post, and there the two remained until the next afternoon, about 2 o'clock, before the water became low enough to permit them to wade. They gradually made their way to the coast, where they obtained assistance, eventually reaching the Grand Isle road, over which they were brought to New Orleans.

Rachel Prince and one daughter were the only members of a colored family of fifteen who were saved, and their home and all it contained was washed away by the flood. Weak from hunger, the old negro woman and her only remaining child stood on the bank and watched the work of the good Samaritans who were dealing out provisions to the white survivors of the storm, without making any attempt to get food and drink from the supplies on the relief boat. Noticing the miserable looking colored people, one of the officers on the boat called: "What do you want, Auntie?"

"Ise hongry, boss, and dis yere chile, de only one de good Lawd spar'd me, is mos' dade for somethin' to eat, sah, but we'se only poor niggers, an dere ain't nothin dere for us, I reckon."

She was told that the provisions were sent to the storm sufferers regardless of race or color, and she should have her share. Then a ham, some pork, tea, coffee, sugar, bread, potatoes and cabbage were given her, and the poor old negro sank down on her knees and while the tears poured over her withered cheeks, she thanked God, and the people who gave charity, for the relief given her.

Emile Delgrante was a young fisherman of Cheniere, of handsome face and form, and a great favorite on the island. For months the young man had looked forward to October 1st, with the most joyful anticipation, for on that day he planned to bring to the home he was making, a bride. A pretty girl who lived on Chandeleur island, a fisherman's daughter, was Emile's sweetheart, and with more than usual ardor the young couple loved each other. Delgrante built him a home, and then spent his leisure hours until his wedding day making it attractive. He made a garden and planted there the flowers his sweetheart loved best, and in the little cot that was to be their home, he

planned all sorts of devices for the comfort and pleasure of his
wife, and when the day dawned that was to make the couple
one, the place made for the bride at Cheniere was unusually
attractive and seemed to the young firsherman, as he took a last
look at it before going for the wife to grace it, a veritable para-
dise.

Delgrante was married and set sail for Cheniere, and on
that fatal Sunday afternoon reached their new home. Many
friends of the couple were there to make them welcome, and several hours were spent in festivity; then the couple were left
alone, for the storm commenced, and every one sought the shelter of his own roof tree.

The happy life planned by those two young lovers was destined to be brief indeed. The tempest howled about their little
home and soon it went to pieces, and Delgrante and his wife
were thrown out into the water that had risen about their house,
and together they perished. The next day their bodies were
found on the beach. They were locked in each other's arms—
united in death as they were in life. One grave was made
for both, and they were laid to rest on the spot where their little cot once stood, and a few feet away, when the tide is in, the
sea waves lap the shore and sound the dirge of the dead lovers,
whose wedding march was a funeral hymn and whose bridal
couch was the grave.

The mother of Capt. John Taylor, an old lady nearly ninety
years old, who lived at Buras, had a narrow escape from death
in the tempest; and the storm of October 1st, was the third that
this old lady had weathered, when many of her neighbors and
kindred found watery graves. She was the only one saved
of the seven children of her mother from the hurricane of 1811;
and in 1831 she was blown in a tree by the furious gale that
devasted a great portion of Louisiana. And to-day she survives
to tell of the horrors of the hurricane of her infancy, the cyclone
of her womanhood and the blast of death of her old age.

An engineer, named Field, on the Fort Jackson and Grand
Isle Railroad, who took a train out soon after the storm, related
his experience. He said all along the track dead animals were
piled so high they had to be removed before the engine could
go along its accustomed route, and near Bonner while directing
the removal of numerous dead animals, a sad spectacle was uncovered. It was the body of a babe lashed to a dead calf, its
little arms still clinging to the animal that went under the waters
and carried it to death instead of to high ground and safety, as
some mother no doubt fondly hoped, when she found all other
chance gone, and bade her darling farewell and trusted to the
animal's instinct to carry it beyond the flood.

One of the women who escaped the fury of the elements at
Cheniere had a terrible experience. She clung to a piece of tim-

ber when the tidal wave swept over the ill-fated island, and was dashed inland at a fearful speed; and then when the wind lulled just before it veered and swept back, washing houses, and dead and living out to sea, she tore up her skirt and catching the limb of a tree, securely lashed her body to it. Other boughs beat her body when the gale recommenced, and great waves broke over her and threatened to drown her where she hung suspended. She saw great trees and timber dashing along, sometimes seeming to be swooping down upon her, then just when she felt her last moment had come, a merciful Providence seemed to intervene, the course of the huge missile would be turned, and hope would once more be renewed in her bosom. Thus she endured the agony of direst terror for five hours, then the water receded, and she was left hanging between Heaven and earth in such a way she could not release herself, and hung thus for a half a day before a party of rescuers found her.

Early on the morn after the tempest a young girl started out from Grand Isle in a pirogue, and cruised about searching among the stacks of dead, rowing close to every dark object she saw floating on the water, and scrutinizing closely everything resembling a body and asking of everyone she met, "Have you seen Freddie?"

Freddie Eichein was her lover, and on that Sunday when the Gulf was churned by the most terrible gale that has swept it for more than half a century, the young fellow was out on a fishing expedition and met the fate of many of his neighbors; he perished in that wind of death, and his body went down to the depths of the sea where no human hands could find it to give it christian burial. Only the darkness of night sent to her home the sweetheart who searched for him, and the first gray of the dawn sent her again on her frantic search for her lover. Her reason tottered, and it is probable for months to come that maid will haunt the waters about Grand Isle hunting for "Freddie."

St. Malo was made up of a colony of Malays, natives of the Malay Archipelago, who had congregated in a village of their own making, beside the waters from which they drew with lines and nets the fish and shrimp that made them a livelihood. They were a happy congregation of good hearted, simple people, who felt, each toward his neighbor, that tender, close feeling of alliance, that all feel toward the people of their own race and country when far from their native land. Many of these people were out on fishing expeditions when the tempest swept over the gulf with such irresistible fury, and they sleep their last sleep in the depths of the waters that has been both their best friend and their worst foe. At St. Malo, the Malay men, women and little ones, had a terrible experience. Their homes were swept away, many of their number were killed, and the survivors are a few desolate mourning people, who have neither homes nor means of making a living, each grief-stricken for the loss of near and dear ones, all seemingly with naught to arouse again ambition to take up life again with any degree of interest.

Carlos Ehring, is one of those who lived to tell of the horrors of that Sabbath night, when St. Malo was wiped from the earth by the tempest that spared so little in its path along the Gulf coast. Ehring says:

AT ST. MALO.

"When the storm came up every one made for my uncle's house, as it was the strongest house on the place. There were sixty people huddled together in the house, men, women and children. Most of the women were praying, and the men were trying to comfort them. My uncle had two children in his arms; he handed me one of the children, a little girl, about two years old. Soon the house began to tremble, and it fell with a crash. I felt a rush of wind, and I ran, I don't know where, but I found myself in the open air. I heard some one calling, and I called and asked who it was, I found that it was John Lewis, a boy sixteen years old. I suddenly thought of an old post, used at one time as a corner post for a house, and I made toward it with the child in my arms. I knew there was a crosspiece on the post. and I climbed toward it. Then I assisted John up the post, wrapping my leg around it, with John under one arm and the baby pressed close to my breast. With the other I clung to the post. The waves rolled over us and the baby cried until exhausted. Poor Johnny was nearly scared to death, but I told him not to be afraid, but to cling to me, which he did.

"There we stayed all night—from 10 o'clock till daybreak next morning. I was terribly stiff and exhausted when I reached the ground. Then I found that the house we had

;THE MALAY HERO.

been in was completely swept away, and that out of the sixty who were in the house the night before we were the sole survivors. I found some whisky and bread, which had been washed under the gallery of the house.

"The child had been crying from hunger, so I soaked the bread in whisky and gave it to the child. I could not eat it myself. About 10 o'clock the lugger Continental hove in sight, and we were taken on board."

Mr. McDonald, son of the mayor of Pass Christian, had a terrible experience, but showed the most remarkable presence of mind recorded during the storm. He was in a sailboat in

front of Biloxi when the gale commenced, and was blown overboard. There were two sailors and a colored boy on the craft,
but they were unable to rescue the young man, for their little
vessel was being blown about like a cork on the angry waves.
The colored boy threw Mr. McDonald a plank, however, and
this he grasped and held to and commenced a wonderful
struggle for life. The waves were mountain high, and he was
dashed along by the furiously driving wind as if but a feather.
He wore a derby hat, and with presence of mind and coolness
that is almost beyond credence, he made the piece of head
gear answer as a life preserver by catching it full of wind and
putting it under his chest. In this way the young man kept
above water for more than an hour, and reached the wreck of
a bridge where he remained until rescued. Mr. McDonald
swam almost nine miles in that fearful storm, with only a piece
of plank and a derby hat to aid him in his magnificent struggle for life.

The strength of the tidal wave may be imagined when it
is known that several porpoises were found in the marsh still
alive at Tropical Bend, four miles from salt water, where they
had been washed by the wave.

A whale, sixteen feet long and weighing several thousand
pounds, was found washed high and dry on a reef, half a mile
west of the West Jetty Light, four days after the storm, and
this wanderer from the deep was still alive and was the object
of much curious scrutiny until some more practical fisherman
came along and killed him to get the oil.

One survivor of the ill-fated Cheniere Caminada was
picked up four days after the storm far out in the Gulf in a
skiff, without oars or sail, and his face bore the unmistakable
imprint of the most terrible suffering. For ninety-six hours
that poor unfortunate had drifted at the mercy of the wind
and waves, scorched by the sun and chilled by the night air,
without water or nourishment except a small catfish which he
caught and ate raw the day before he was rescued.

One of the saddest and most startling sights that met the
band that penetrated the swamps after the storm in search of
wounded and dead was the corpse of Mrs. Geo. Danton. Deep
in the swamps, where the trees grow so close together their
boughs were intertwined and made a roof of green that kept
out sun and rain, save in one spot where a giant oak stood in a
small clear space, she was found. A beam of sunlight found
its way across a limb of the oak, which was about ten feet from
the ground, and there, showing in clear relief, in that one ray
of light in the dark forest, was Mrs. Danton, hanging by a
tress of her long, raven black hair to the limb, her body perfectly nude, her eyes wide open, with the look of horror in
them that froze there by the chill of death when she saw the

pandemonium about her and realized her death was inevitable in that furious hurricane.

The experience of Joseph Frelich, the little Austrian hero, could not be told in more beautiful language than that of the report of his story as follows, by the New Orleans Times-Democrat of Oct. 7. It is one of the most pathetic incidents of that terrible storm:

"Joseph Frelich is a hero. With his father and friends he had found the remains of his mother during the day, and when found by the reporter had just come from her resting place. The body had been brought in late, not being found until nearly 6 o'clock. The sad scenes at the last resting place are described elsewhere. The lad, a mere child, had passed through experiences within a few days that would age him more than years of natural life. His home was at Bayou Cook. There had been seven in the family—father, mother, three brothers and two sisters. All were at home Sunday night when the awful visitation came. Their camp was blown down about 10 o'clock in the evening. Joe and Rosalie had been always the most friendly of brothers and sisters. It was his pride and joy to do for Rosalie all that in older persons would have been termed the offices of lovers. She was his darling and his pet, and when this evening came all his love and devotion and all hers were shown. But in how sorrowful and how tender a way. The records of the world might be searched without finding more heroism than was shown by these simple fisher folks' children amid all the horrors and darkness of the night. She had given up her life that her brother might be saved! He was to her the type and acme of all that was to be sought as well as her best beloved blood relative. When the camp was blown down and all were struggling for very life in the wild and raging waters, Joe looked for Rosalie. They had been separated in the blowing down of the dwelling. Rosalie also had her favorite brother in mind and when they found one another in the darkness, with glad cries they clasped arms and Joe guided her to where a piece of the roof was out of the raging current and a little shelter was afforded. Soon their frail and insufficient support was swept from them, and here Joe began the story which, were it known broadcast over this land would render him and his little dead sister famous: 'I cried to Rosalie when the pieces of roof to which we were clinging were lost to us to put her arms around my neck and hold tight and fast to me. This she did. No fear was shown by the little darling. She was as brave and as much composed as at any ordinary time.

Many a time have I had her out in my boats, and she knew the water well; she knew me well too. Once she had me strong and good I shouted to her, for notwithstanding we were only a few inches apart, such was the howling of the gale that no ordinary tones could be heard, to slip up on my back as I struck out to swim, and that I would save us both. She smiled at me and pulling my head down kissed me twice. I'll never forget how beautiful she looked as she gazed into my eyes for what was the last time. Having twisted herself about and securing a firm clasp of her arms around my neck, she shouted in my ear : 'Joe, darling, now go quick. I'll help you all I can.'

"Off we were, and water all over us, down into the seething and boiling waves. Sometimes under, sometimes, for a brief time, on the surface ; but we kept up and I began to have hope. Big logs came swirling and hissing by us and we were nearly forced apart, but still we struggled on. It was nearly a mile to land from where we started. We must have been in the water half an hour when I was becoming weak and faint. I am a good swimmer and the Mississippi River never had a better one," and everybody gathered around knew the lad was telling the truth, "but the pressure of sister's arms around my neck had interfered with my breathing, which, under any circumstances, would have been hard enough, and I was short of wind. I began to go deeper and deeper into the foul water ; each time it was more and more difficult to recover myself and dimness and darkness seemed to be rushing through my eyes. Rosalie noticed it. She let go one hand and tried in a weak way to help me buffet the waters; but alas ! we were making less and less headway. 'Joe, Joe, good-by darling : good-bye forever,' she shouted to me. 'Save yourself. Good-by, good-by !' and she was gone. She had voluntarily sacrificed herself to save me. I caught for her hair, which had become loosened and was floating like a beautiful mass of the ivy moss. I could not reach her and she swept by me. I saw her sink and with all my remaining strength I dived down into the black waters. I couldn't see a thing under the water, and my strength gone, nearly strangled and exhausted, I came to the surface. Rosalie had gone. She was drowned before my eyes and I couldn't save her. There can't be a good Lord. He never would have allowed it." And the lad broke down and wept. No wonder. Fresh from the grave of a beloved mother and the scenes of his struggle for the life of his only love, brought vividly before him by the recital of the tale, were too much, and by kindly friends he was led away to be taken care of by sympathizing and generous neighbors. The body of Rosalie has been recovered."

A tale of horrible suffering was told by a party that were rescued at Southwest Pass, four days after the storm:

The party was as follows: Leon Torrio, Paul Gautrie, A. Terrebonne, Andre Colon, Alcide Pinsene, Dupre Terrebonne,

O. Terrebonne, Joseph Bonette, Alcide Bonnette Alexis Croby, an American, named Gaspard, an Australian and three Malays. The American, Australian and Malays were picked up in Bayou Andre. The others came from Cheniere. These unfortunates were all in Torio's house when the wave came that carried the house away and threw them into the sea. They say that just before the storm the wind was from the east. Then it lulled and the water began to rise very rapidly and the house of Torrio was swept away. The nine men clung to planks and doors and managed to bind their frail supports together in the form of a raft, and on this they floated out to sea and met the party from Bayou Andre and they floated about for four days before they reached the Pass and received succor. Their bodies were parched and swollen and they were so haggard and weak they presented a most pitiful appearance. All they had to subsist on for ninety-six hours had been the dead rats and animals that floated near enough their raft to be reached by the starving men, and not a drop of water had passed the parched lips of the unfortunates since they had been swept out into the storm-lashed waters the Sunday night, four days before their rescue.

The following is from the New Orleans Times-Democrat of Oct. 8:

"Among the passengers who arrived on the Grand Isle train, a week after the storm, were two Slavonian fishermen, Matthew Culuz and Matthew Rumarich. These men were five days clinging to an upturned boat, floating in the Gulf of Mexico without a mouthful of food or a drop of water. Emaciated and bruised, with sunken eyes, hollow cheeks and the skin peeled off their faces in large patches, they presented a pitable appearance. The men's clothing consisted of a suit of underclothing, every other garment having been lost during the great storm.

On their arrival they were taken in charge by the Slavonian Society and furnished with clothing and medical attendance. The men were seen at the store of Mr. Baccich by a Times-Democrat reporter. They were hardly able to talk, owing to their tongues being swollen from the terrible sufferings undergone. What could be gathered from their incoherent talk would furnish a tale of suffering and distress which would rival any of the best stories of our best writers of naval fiction, the difference only being that in the case of these men it is a demonstrated fact, the condition of the men showing plainly that theirs is no ordinary tale of suffering.

The man Culuz, when he arrived, was not recognized by his most intimate friends around the French Market.

From a stout hearty man of 165 pounds, straight as an arrow, he is now bowed down, with stooping shoulders, and a look of despair on a face which must have had an intelligent look before the present awful experience. His present weight is 132 pounds, a falling off of 33 pounds in five days. His companion, Matthew Rumarich, is a swarthy heavy built man, with a full beard, and twinkling brown eyes, which have not lost their lustre, notwithstanding the hardships undergone in the last few days. He did not appear to suffer as much as his companion, although he complains of his chest feeling sore and a difficulty of breathing.

MATHEW RUMARICH and MATHEW KULUZ.

The men were in their fishing camp on Razor Island, in Grand Lake, in the early part of last Sunday's storm, and while the water was rising the men, realizing that it was m ore than an ordinary storm, pulled up the floor of the camp to keep the building from floating away. Ere this work was finished the water was several feet deep in the camp. They sought refuge in the loft of the house, thinking the building would weather the gale. In this they were disappointed, as in a short time the building gave way and they were buried among the ruins. Fortunately the house broke up and each managed to secure a piece of the wreck. They became separated and Rumarich came in contact with a submerged skiff, which he caught hold of, abandoning the rude raft. Culuz also floated close to the skiff, and guided by his companion's cries, managed to join him.

All night long they clung to the skiff, buffetted by the waves and drifting they knew not whither. When morning dawned they were terrified to find that they had drifted out of sight of land and were in the open Gulf. The wind had calmed down considerably, but the sea, as usual, after a storm, was running high and they were still obliged to exert all their strength to keep hold of their frail support. Finding that the heavy clothes they wore were an impediment to them, holding them in the water, they began the work of stripping themselves. This was no easy task, with the waves carrying their little craft first high on a wave and then dashing them with hurricane force into a trough of the sea. All day Monday the men clung to the boat, keeping a sharp lookout for a passing vessel.

Monday night came and went and the sun rose on Tuesday with still no change in their dreadful situation. All day Tuesday the men held on, still hoping against hope, and although their bodies were sore and every muscle ached they still clung to their only support. Through the long hours of Tuesday night the men tried to cheer one another, and both kept a lookout, with the delusive hope that a passing vessel would come close enough to hear their cries. Wendesday came and the real suffering of the men commenced. With a hot sun beating down on them and the salt spray flying over their uncovered backs, their skin commenced to blister and peel off, leaving the raw, tender flesh beneath.

Over the raw flesh the waves would wash; the sun then coming down would still further aggravate their misery. Added to this they were intensely thirsty and weak from their long fast.

After dark on Thursday, probably about 9 o'clock, Rumarich cried out to his companion in their native tongue: " *Nvala Bogu ero, svjetlos*"—"Thank God, here is a light." True enough, there before them was a lighthouse, and as they had often sailed around it they recognized it as being the lighthouse at Southwest Pass. The wind was blowing then directly toward the light and they looked on their deliverance as being near at hand. Slowly they drifted towards the light and were already thanking God for their escape when suddenly the wind freshened and veered round to another direction and the seemingly doomed men were again driven out to sea.

Culuz then gave way in despair and loosened his hold of the boat. His companion caught him by the hair and dragged him back to the skiff, saying: *"Nebojse."* "Dont fear we shall be saved yet." After that Rumarich had to use his best persuasive powers to induce his companion to retain his hold. Twice Culuz cast himself adrift and each time he was caught by his spirited shipmate.

It was well that he did not abandon the craft, for deliverance was, unknown to them, close at hand.

Early Friday morning, at about 2 o'clock, as near as they could judge, their feet touched bottom and they waded ashore. In walking around the island they saw the light of a lugger, lying about a quarter of a mile from the island.

One of the men, Culuz, although weak and exhausted, undertook to swim to the lugger, being fearful of taking the chance of waiting till morning. He reached the lugger safely and immediately a boat was dispatched for his companion. Before the boat reached the beach, Michel Sacanogao, who was hunting lost friends, pulled to the beach and took off Rumarich. They were taken by the Louisiana, the rescuing boat, and cared for.

Thursday two men were at the landing at Gretna awaiting a boat that was en route to Cheniere. One was white faced, haggard and desperate looking and when the boat arrived he took passage, after bidding his companion an affectionate farewell. The appearance of the man who had left was such that inquiry was made of the other as to his identity, and the cause of his grief stricken appearance. The man refused to give his name, but said, "It is my brother you saw me tell good-bye. He has gone to Cheniere, and I shall never see him again, never. His wife and five children perished in the storm, and everything he possessed of earthly value was swept away by the wind and waves, and he has gone to commit suicide on the spot where his loved ones met their sad fate."

The men were not alone in their deeds of daring and self-sacrifice, women, in many instances, showed wonderful presence of mind and fortitude. Mrs. Barbier, the wife of Capt. John Barbier, whose camp is on Grand Bayou, proved herself one of the heroines that were developed in that night of terror, devastation and death. Her husband was in New Orleans, and she was at their home with her five small children, the eldest but nine years old, when the storm commenced. The little ones became panic stricken when the wind shrieked above the house like an army of demons; and when the waters rose beneath the building and upheaved the floor, it was only by the greatest effort Mrs. Barbier succeeded in getting her children on the only piece of floor that remained—a small fragment in one corner. Just as she pulled one frightened little fellow to her, the baby she had clasped in her arms, was swept from her, and she never saw it again; its little body was dashed among the debris, and went to swell the list of those who found unknown graves. The house was unusually strong and stood the tempest, and all night that mother stood in water up to her breast and managed to keep the heads of her other children above the waves, while she mourned the loss of her babe which was swept, only God knows whither.

At Savoy there is a house denuded of its eaves. The wind shaved them off as cleanly as if some giant instrument had been used, yet left the house itself otherwise uninjured.

George Seferovich had a terrible experience. The big waves from the Gulf rent his home in bits and threw him, his wife and two children into the foaming, storm-lashed waters. Before his very eyes he saw a huge piece of timber crush his wife, the mother of the two children he was struggling to save. He heard the wails of his little ones for the mother they loved, and his own heart echoed their cries, yet he fought for life for the sake of his little ones. One child climbed on his back and clung round his neck, but finding the huge waves that ever and anon broke over them, were strangling the child, he seized it by its clothing with the same hand that held up the other, and struggled toward a tree. When that haven was almost reached, a big cypress log swooped down upon them, and struck the child who he was supporting by its dress. The brave Austrian felt the shock of the awful blow it received, and he longed, yet feared, to learn the extent of his darling's injuries. The wind shrieked above them and the rain beat upon them fiercely, and almost exhausted, Seferovich pulled himself and his children up into the tree. Then he looked into the face of the child who had been struck by the cypress log. It shown white in the darkness, and no heaving of the tiny bosom told the anxious father that his darling still lived. The form of the little one stiffened in his grasp. Its soul had winged its flight to the mother, gone just before. All night the brave Austrian hugged the bodies of the dead and the living child; and there he was found in the morning, stupid with grief and exhaustion.

Francoise La France, a man of magnificent phisique, and wonderful strength by reason of his tall, well proportioned stature, and muscles that were hardened by daily toil, saved his wife and four children from the ruin of their home at Riceland, but his first born, a sturdy little fellow, who was the pride of his parents, met his death in a horrible manner. When the roof began to cave in, Mr. La France called to his family to leave the building, and himself caught the rafters and heavy boards on his broad back, and prevented their crushing his wife and younger children. When he supposed his dear ones were all out of his home he struggled out into the storm himself and hurried with his family to the home of his nearest neighbor where his first exclamation, as he staggered across the threshold, was "Thank God we are all saved." But the mother's eye missed one from the number of her family. Michel, the oldest boy, was not there. Back through the fierce wind and driving rain the frightened parents went, accompanied by their neighbors. The work of removing the wreck and searching for the lad was commenced in the dark, with the mother's wails to urge them on to their task. Finally, the little fellow was found, pinned down by heavy timbers, and just as his crushed body was discerned some one appeared with a lantern, and its yellow light fell across the mangled form and showed the mother her boy pinned to the earth, with one eye squeezed from the socket, and one little hand extended, and fast stiffening in the clasp of death, with a rafter across it, that showed the flesh and bone crushed to a pulp when it was removed. After the child was taken from the wreck he was carried by his father, followed by the mother, whose cries could be heard above the din of the storm, and the sympathizing friends who went with them to the house they thought would be a haven of safety for all, until the boy was missed. The next morning, a rough pine box was made, and the mangled body was laid in it and carried to a spot of high ground and laid to sleep, the sleep eternal, with only the sobs of his mother and the dull thuds of spads patting the earth on other graves all about to break the depressing silence that hovered about that scene of desolation.

Charles Dennette, a negro, who lived at Happy Jack, fifty miles from New Orleans, was in his humble home when the wind became furious, and his family clung to him and begged to be protected from the "wrath of ole Marster." The roof of the house was blown off and carried into a neighboring cornfield and Dennette bade his family get out of doors as the house was sure to fall upon them if they did not leave it. All but two of the family escaped to the yard before their home caved in, but two children were crushed beneath the fallen timbers, and then were cremated by the fire that started among the debris. The rushing winds fanned the flames until, but a few moments later, nothing remained to Dennette of his home or the two children burned with it,—not even the ashes, for they were blown far and wide.

Among those who were doomed by that fatal storm was a gentlemen from New York, whose name is not known, for all those who had been wont to associate with him passed beyond the possibility of giving their evidence. He came from the North, and left his home and kindred who were dear to him, to seek health in the balmy southland. The breezes of mild temperature at Cheniere had wooed back to the stranger the strength he sought, and he lingered with the people who had been his companions for a half a year, because he had grown attached to them and their beautiful land, and he was slow to bid farewell to the scenes where he had found health and strength. But the storm came and is now but a memory, and the family of the stranger in the far North will look in vain for his return. He will go home never more. His body rests with a host of others in a shallow grave dug by a band of good Samaritans who laid to rest the victims of the great storm. Instead of gaining a new lease of life down among the orange trees and salt breezes, the northern stranger met death and an unknown grave,—death in a strange land with no loved one near, the sad fate the Hindoo ever fears, and that he prays may not befall his friends in his benediction "may you die among your kindred."

Near Fort Jackson the receding waters left a sad spectacle for the band of rescuers who came that way soon after the storm. Caught in a barbed wire fence were the bodies of three little girls, sisters no doubt, for the same brown curls clustered around the faces of each, and the features were strongly similar. Each held one hand of the other in a close death grip, and they were not separated by those who dug the shallow grave in which they were placed. Side by side the little girls were laid upon a litter of planks, and green boughs covered forever the sweet faced dead children who went together over Death's river, and the strong men who piled the boughs above their bodies were not ashamed of the tears that trickled down their rough cheeks as they buried, without coffins, shroud or burial service, some mother's darlings, some father's pride.

When the first light dawned of the coming day that was to reveal in all its hideousness the desolation and ruin created during the darkness of that Sabbath night, Mr. Fred Stockfleth heard a plaintive sobbing out in the shadows of a pile of debris that was being tossed by the falling waters. Wondering if there could be any living being among that stack of wreckage, he called "Is any one there?" and a weak baby voice sobbed "I is," and another childish tone added, "and me." There were not many minutes between the time when those little ones were heard crying miserably out on the dark water, that was ruffled by the cold morning air, until brave Fred. Stockfleth pushed his way on a plank, to their sides. There, crouched on a huge log, were two children, a boy and a girl: the boy, who was evidently two or three years older than his little sister, was about eight years of age. With one arm around the shoulders of the sister whose long blonde curls were crushed against his shoulder, that little fellow had alternately begged "don't cry, sister," and then sobbed pitifully himself, for hours, while the log on which they drifted was many times almost careened or sunk, by others. Their baby tongues lisped this broken story to Mr. Stockfleth, of some of their trials out in the darkness and danger of that night, but neither could tell what their names were. Only "sister," and "buzzer" had they been taught to call each other, and when an effort was made to learn what name their parents were called by,

the cries of the children for "Mamma" and "Papa," were so piti-
iful their new friends desisted in their efforts to learn their identity; and unless some acquaintance sees and recognizes these little waifs of the storm they will have to go through life without
the knowledge of father, mother or kindred, unacquainted even
with their own name.

Nick Salotich and John Perovich, two of the survivors,
worked among the injured and buried the dead near their camp
on Bayou Cook, all Monday, and late in the evening rejoiced in
the discovery of some hard tack and fresh water, which they
found in a portion of a wrecked lugger. On this meagre refresh-
ment they subsisted until Wednesday, when it gave out, and they
started toward the city for succor. They had not proceeded far
when they discovered two objects on the sandy beach, weakly
moving, and hurried to discover who the beings were, and to
help them, if possible. They found Nicholas Micisich, and John
Descovich, both bereft of their reason. These unfortunates had
managed to save themselves from the watery grave their families
found, but their fate was far worse than if they had succumbed
to the wind of the hurricane of three evenings previous, for
they had been so bruised and battered they found strength only
to descend to the beach the next morning, and there they had
lain for three days. The limbs of the tree to which they
clung through that night of terror, had bruised and battered
their bodies, and broken their bones, leaving only a remnant
of life that would have been better taken. The sun the
next day shone brightly on their bodies from which the clothes
had all been torn off, and their flesh scorched and blistered
in the heat, and their blood coursed madly through their
veins from the fever that slowly consumed their vitality.
Their tongues parched and swelled and cracked and hung
bleeding from their mouths, and their eyes almost burst from
their sockets; and while their voices lasted, they buried their
bruised hands in the sand, in excess of agony, and cried aloud
for water. Visions of pools of the life-giving elixir that is
brewed in the clouds floated before them, but while they vainly
struggled to reach the limpid depths that would have been to
them the greatest boon, like the mirages of the desert, they
kept ever just beyond reach and goaded them to madness.
Springs seemed to gush up from the burning sands beside
them, and the cool waters sparkled in the sunlight, and the
spray, like a vail of mist between, seemed almost to dash in
in their very faces; but when they put out their hands
for just the few drops · their palms would have held,
the spring vanished; they were but the result of their
fevered fancy. Night came, and the stars looked down on
them, and to the bloodshot eyes of the crazed men, seemed
like fiery torches that added to their fever, and yet failed to

keep them from shivering when the night air struck their nude and burning bodies. They raved aloud until their tongues became so swollen they could not speak, then their senses left them—they became insane. In this awful plight they were found Wednesday evening by Salovich and Perovich. Human help came too late to relieve the agonies of Macisich. A few moments after he was found, his swollen, blackened body was relieved of pain by the Master's hand. He was dead. Descovich lived to reach a neighboring camp where he was carried

Sisters of Charity on Picayune Relief Boat.

by his rescuers, and food and water were given him, and physicians who saw him later say he will probably recover his strength, but his mind, never. His reason has forever forsaken him.

Capt. Elie Peters and Philip Peters, of the schooner Rescue, had a sad and thrilling experience. The vessel capsized in the early hours of Monday morning, and Capt. Peters and his brothers Allan and Philip clung to a piece of lumber, from which they were repeatedly washed until they succeeded in getting on to a piece of square timber and were carried out to sea. They were at the mercy of the waves for three days and nights. On Wednesday Allan gave out and went down. On the evening of the same day Capt. Peters saw the waterlogged lugger Raphael Raymo, of New Orleans, with two young men on board. He and Philip got on board the lugger and bailed her out, rigged up a sail from some old canvas, and steered her as best they could, her rudder being lost. This work took until Thursday morning. They were exposed to the elements four days and nights without food or water except two cans of tomatoes found on the lugger and a little rain water licked up from the deck. To Capt. Peters is due the saving of Philip and the two young men on the lugger, as well as himself. He repeatedly helped his brother Allan back on the stick of timber when the seas would wash him off, often letting go and swimming out after him, but all to no purpose. He kept Philip with him to the last, and by his courage and fortitude managed the lugger until land was reached. The two youths in the lugger had abandoned all hope and given up.

In one place a lugger was found after the storm in a dense forest more than a mile from the water, where it had been carried over the tree tops on that great tidal wave, and left were it now stands. To launch it again, a road would have to be chopped through the woods, and the vessel would have to be hauled overland for a mile before it could be floated again. The appearance of a big lugger resting in the midst of a dense forest, where no human skill could have carried it, is novel. It must have been carried on the water above the tops of the tall trees, and then left where it now is, and allowed to gradually settle down to the earth as the water receded.

In what is left of the handsome orange orchard of Louis Clugigola, toward the northwestern portion of Grand Isle, there were seen and recognized the fragments of furniture and household goods from Cheniere Caminada, while above them in the wind-whipped leafless branches of the trees were fluttering the tattered fragments of little children's clothes that had been driven some six miles from the Cheniere, grim and sorrowful reminders of the cold and merciless impartiality of that terrible cyclone.

There was but one white person drowned on Grand Isle, although the tempest blew with such terrific force over the resort it levelled to the earth almost everything there, and when the water from the sea swept over it, houses and hotels, trees and furniture were carried out in the Gulf. Several colored people perished on the island, but Madame Victor Rigaud, was the only white person there who was sacrificed to the warring elements during that storm that will doubtless prevent Grand Isle from ever again attracting the idle pleasure seekers to its shores. She was a highly respected old lady who had first seen the light on the island, and who had seldom left it during her lifetime. She was the wife of one of the descendants of Lafitte's crew, and the couple lived in a house that was over a hundred years old, and which contained many relics of a bygone pirate's collection of curios and handsome spoil that fell to his share from looting expeditions, among them five copies from originals by Raphael and Le Brun. Only six weeks before the storm a Northern visitor offered the old man $4000 cash for the five paintings, and he refused to sell them. They had been in the family, he said, for generations, and no amount of money could buy them. He valued them because they were valuable, but more because they were heirlooms. When the storm came the old man gave his attention to his own life and his wife's. They both clung to the roof of their house as long as they could, but Madam Rigaud was swept off and drowned.

The name of Lawrence Lawson, the lighthouse keeper at Grand Isle, should be preserved as a hero, for that night when the winds beat down houses and trees that had weathered a century's storms, and sent to the depths of the sea, sturdy vessels that never before were injured by the tempests of the deep, brave Lawrence Lawson stood to his perilous post of duty when it seemed as if his allegiance to his task must be met with death. In the teeth of the gale, with the roar and rush of the wind about the lighthouse, sounding like the booming of cannon, and above it the shrieks of the people who were being dashed to death, the keeper climbed the narrow stair-way and kept burning the light that shone far out on the boiling waters, and that gleamed, a beacon of hope, to the struggling beings who were being tossed about on the seething waves; and many there were who say that but for that one light that shone in the black of that stormy night, they must have perished. But ever and anon as they rose to the top of some foam crested wave, they saw the beacon beaming and renewed their grasp of the plank or tree that kept them from the jaws of death. The people of Grand Isle speak the name of Lawrence Lawson reverently, and agree that he played the part of a hero in his performance of duty that awful night, and strong men and little children send aloft in their prayers to the Almighty petitions for the Divine blessing to ever rest on this noble, fearless fellow.

Of the family of which Mme. Sandras and her cousin, John Valence, were members, they alone survive, of their fifty odd kinspeople who lived with them at Cheniere Caminada.

The pilot boat Underwriter picked up Gladimer Lafond, a fourteen year old boy, eighteen miles off South Pass lighthouse, eight days after the storm. The poor little fellow was in a pitiable condition, having drifted about on a plank in the Gulf eight days without food or water. He was unconscious when found, and not until liquor had been poured down his throat did he show any sign of life, and then he only roused sufficiently to give his name and age, and to say he, with his father and mother had lived at Cheniere, and they had taken refuge on a lugger when the storm burst in its fury, and the vessel had been capsized by the wind, and he alone was left to tell the tale.

Mr. Mendona's house was demolished, but a cabin in the rear withstood the attack of wind and waves. He was absent on a trip to the city for provisions when fhe relief boat visited his place, but his wife, Constantin, a very handsome and educated lady, who spoke excellent English, told a graphic story of the storm to a Times-Democrat reporter: She with her daughter, Mathilda, a beautiful little dark-eyed miss of ten years, and her sister were in the house when the storm came on a little before 9 o'clock. From the manner in which the big house swayed and shook during the storm, they quickly determined that their only chance of escape lay in retreating to the smaller cabin. The water was dashing over the high gallery that connected the two buildings, but they clung to the narrow walk as they crawled along on their hands and knees, and finally reached the cabin, hardly knowing how they did so. They fastened the doors and windows tightly, feeling that they had made they last stand against despair and death.

"We can only pray," said Constantin Mendoza to her sister and daughter. The swaying of the cabin had thrown the clock and the lighted lamp, which stood on the same shelf, half way across the room and they were in blackest darkness, fearing every moment that the great waves, which were now making clean breaches over the roof, would bring it down upon their heads, while the immense volume of water that was rolling under the house threatened to burst open the floor or tear the whole structure in pieces. Mrs. Mendoza groped about for matches, and ultimately finding them, she lit the candles on the little alter, and setting the example herself, she exhorted the others to pray for divine aid. The altar was only a little cracker box, neatly cover with wall paper, having a crucifix and decorated with scriptural pictures.

It was firmly fixed to the wall and when the candles within it had been lighted they threw a dim shaft of pale yellow light into the thick and almost palpable darkeess of the room. Then, with the wind striking wildly as it swept through the inky darkness of that awful night, the mountainous waves roaring and thundering on the trembling beach and lashing the slender walls of the cabin till they bent and fluttered like the sails of a schooner in a tempest, these three dark-eyed women knelt upon the heaving, quivering floor, right in the path of that shaft of yellow light and it strangely illumined their dark oval faces, which seemed to come out of the surrounding darkness with an effect weirdly suggestive of the supernatural.

Then came a demand for further action. With a small hatchet they chopped the thin board flooring and soon they were waist deep in the heaving water. The black waves rose and fell as they lapped and splashed the furniture in the dark corners of the room, but still the candles, set deep in the altar

TIMES–DEMOCRAT RELIEF BOAT

their flames almost touching the crucifix, threw that shaft of dim yellow light out upon the dark heaving water that threatened to swallow them up, and still, though chilled to the heart with terror and bitter cold and deafened by the dreadful roaring of the hungry seas as they thundered along the low-lying beach and swept across the broad levels of sea marsh, they turned their pale faces up to that dim light, while their blue and quivering lips moved in prayer. Thus they prayed and wept and waited for dawn. It came at last and the storm passed away with the darkness. Though the tempest had swept away about all that thrift, industry and good fortune had converted into a happy and prosperous home for the Mendoza family, they were happy and thankful that Monday morning's sun brought to them the knowledge that no breach had been made in the home circle.

Perhaps one of the most thrilling experiences of the storm was told by a woman who drifted in to shore lashed to a log. She, her husband and two children had taken refuge on board a schooner anchored outside of Bayou Cook, and intended to ride out the gale. When the wind came from the west, followed by a mammoth wave, the husband and two children were washed overboard, and the lugger's mast, snapping off at its foot, drifted from the side of the vessel. The frantic woman jumped for the floating timber and in some way lashed herself to it. All night she drifted through Adam's bayou and the neighboring bays, and when daylight came she was picked up by the lugger Venus. She was brought to Mr. Fred Stockfleth's, half naked, starved and terribly bruised about the body, and half crazed with grief for the loss of her husband and children.

Villechere Vinet, who lived on Bayou Challon, with his father, mother and brother, took refuge on a raft, and they were tossed about all through that night of terror, in the darkness, wind and rain. When the day dawned, the father caught a pirogue that floated near, and entered it to go for aid for his family. He had not gone two boat lengths when the frail craft overturned, and the father went down to rise no more. The mother sprang to the edge of the raft and waited several minutes, gazing on the water for the re-appearance of her life companion, but he was fast in the sea weed in the depths beneath. Then she leaped into the bayou and was again united with her husband, this time on the shores of Eternity, to part never more. The eldest son seeing both parents drown, leaped from the raft, and he, too, found a watery grave, leaving only the last member of the family, the boy Villechere, to tell the story. He was picked up several hours later, dazed with grief and half dead from exhaustion.

There is but one member of Emile Prosperi's family of sixteen to tell how the storm beat against their home and the fate it meted out to the others. A boy ten years old is the survivor. He, with his father, mother, brothers and sisters were seated about a table on which a lamp burned brightly, lighting the pages of the old family bible from which the father read the usual evening lesson to his family. The wind howled more fiercely as verse after verse of the good Book was read, until the voice, that told the story of the death that gave to mankind hope beyond the grave, was drowned by the war of the tempest. The house trembled and swayed as the great tidal wave rose rapidly beneath and around it and beat against its walls. Stricken with sudden terror the family rushed toward the attic, but the ten year old boy who survived, was slower of motion than the rest, and to this fact he owes his life. Before he reached the stairway the other members of his family had ascended, the floor was upheaved, and before he realized what was happening, he was borne out on the flood, and into a tree a hundred yards beyond. Then he saw a tiny flame shoot up from the half collapsed building then another and another, until, in a few moments the wild scene about was illumined by the flames, that started by the overturned lamp, enveloped Prosperi's home. The cries of the family penned in the garret were borne above the howling of the tempest, and the boy in the tree clung to the branches and watched the burning funeral pyre of his loved ones, and was found by a rescuing party the next day.

Mrs. Frank Kranz, Jr., a daughter-in-law of the hotel proprietor of Grand Isle, lost one hundred and fifty relatives in the storm. Among them was her sister, the wife of John Valence, of Cheniere Caminada. When the survivors at stricken Cheniere were counted Mrs. Valence, who was shortly expected to become a mother, was missing. Her body could not be found, and she was enrolled among those who had found a grave in the waters of the gulf, or whose bones were bleaching in the trackless sea-marsh of the shore. Five weeks after the storm the crew of a lugger dancing over the dimpling waters of the gulf descried a dark spot on the blue water twenty miles from land. The lugger's course was altered and it bore down upon the object. As it approached the crew made out the object to be a raft and on it a motionless figure; its dress proclaimed it a woman, its posture announced it dead. But these fishermen resolved to give it christian burial and took the raft in tow and made for land.

By the clothing the body was recognized as that of Mrs. Valence. Swept to sea on that awful night, she had managed, in her desperate struggle for her own life and that of her unborn babe, to gather a few planks of the wreckage and construct the rude raft upon which her body was found. The thought of this helpless woman alone, in her condition, upon that night of death, was awful enough, but when tender hands sought to lift

the emaciated body from the few planks which bore it up, the
full horror of her fate was seen. By her side lay the naked
body of a new born babe. On a frail support of a few rough
planks, tossed on the waters of a storm lashed sea, with the demon of the storm as the only attendant, that young life was
ushered into the world, to die. What pen can paint, what
imagination can picture, the awful fate of that helpless woman,
slowly starving to death on that awful expanse of water with the
wails of her famished babe ringing in her ears? Mother and
child had perished from starvation.

Archie Williamson, A Hero of Caminada.

While the storm was raging on that awful night and death
was riding abroad on the wings of the wind the crossing of the
electric wires in the city of New Orleans caused the fire bells to
ring continuously through the night. Not with the rapid
clangor of the fire alarm, but with the slow and measured toll
of the "passing bell." The weirdness of that eerie sound cannot
be imagined, much less described.

Borne on the pinions of the rushing wind each mournful
stroke smote on the hearing of the startled listener with a funeral sound, ominous of disaster. And so it proved. The latest
found element of nature tolled the knell of the hundreds of victims who, on bay and bayou, in marsh, swamp and prairie, on
the shores of the river, the coasts of the gulf and the isles of the
sea, were falling before that awful Wind of Death.

FINIS.